Oysterback Spoken Here

Oysterback Spoken Here

by

Helen Chappell

Illustrations by
Rick Kollinger

Introduction by
Tom Horton

WOODHOLME
HOUSE
PUBLISHERS

Baltimore, Maryland

© 1998   Helen Chappell

Printed and bound in the United States of America.

1 2 3 4 5   07 06 05 04 03 02 01 00 99 98

Library of Congress Cataloging-in-Publication Data

Chappell, Helen
   Oysterback spoken here / by Helen Chappell; Illustrations by Rick Kollinger
      p.   cm.
   ISBN 1-891521-01-2 (pbk.)
   1. Chesapeake Bay Region (Md. and Va.)—Social life and customs—Fiction.
   2. Eastern Shore (Md. and Va.)—Social life and customs—Fiction. 3. City
   and town life—Maryland—Fiction. I. Title.
   PS3553.H299096   1998
   813'.54—dc 21   98-16063
                                                     CIP

Woodholme House Publishers
1829 Reisterstown Road
Suite 130
Baltimore, Maryland 21208
E-mail: whp@ix.netcom.com
Fax: (410) 653-7904
Orders: 1-800-488-0051

Cover and book design: Lance Simons
Cover illustration: Rick Kollinger

Portions of the book previously appeared in slightly altered form in the *Baltimore Sun*.

In Loving Memory
of Blanche Chappell

AKNOWLEDGMENTS

Hal Piper is my Max Perkins, my *Sun* editor *extraordinaire*. Without him, Oysterback would be a long-forgotten trunk novel and I'd be stocking pet food at Wal-Mart, but he took a chance and we had a great nine years. Thank you, Hal. Long may you edit.

Thanks also to other *Sun* folk, past and present: Jim Bready, Patricia Fanning, Jacques Kelly, Marilyn McCraven, Michele Pratka, Steve Proctor, Dan Rodricks, and Jerry Sullivan. And to the Geezers Club; long may you geeze.

Gregg Wilhelm, my Woodholme House editor, deserves my thanks for his faith and hard work, and also for championing the cause of small presses everywhere. Thanks also to Brian and Elizabeth Weese, my publishers, for their vision of what a small press should be and can be. I am grateful to Gregg, Brian, and Liz for making this work a part of that vision.

Thanks to Lance Simons for his delightful design, from his choice of fonts to his unique conceptualization of "The Bugeye" newspaper pages.

Thanks to my old friend and fellow unindicted co-conspirator Rick Kollinger, whose fine visual hand can be seen in every aspect of Oysterback from column to play to book. Free speech rules!

Thanks also to Tom Horton, Abigail Horton, and Imogene Horton and all the Horton family who have made me feel like one of them. And what a great family to be a part of!

I am especially indebted to John Barth. To have the accolades of a writer who has been a seminal influence on my own paltry work is more than I ever dreamed possible.

To all the fine Eastern Shore folks from the West Side to Tilghman to Fishing Creek to Chestertown who have played a role in making Oysterback the town it is, many thanks for laughing instead of killing me. You know who you are. And if you don't, maybe it's just as well.

Last, but certainly not least, a thousand thanks to all of Oysterback's loyal readers and fans. Without you, Oysterback would just be a piney cripple in the marsh. Keep the faith.

Contents

AN EERIE VISIT TO OYSTERBACK

TOM HORTON

One day, I paddled my kayak into a creek where the charts showed no creek existed. Night was coming on, and though it was clear and starry ahead, an odd fog blotted everything astern, pushing me ever deeper into the Dorchester marshes.

No town existed in these parts, but around a bend I came upon a fishing village. I glided silently past a dock where two shadowy figures were deep in conversation:

"Think on this, Huddie," said the one called Junie. "If an infinite number of rednecks, driving an infinite number of pickup trucks, fires an infinite number of shotguns at an infinite number of road signs—would they eventually reproduce all the world's great literature in Braille?"

It was not your average waterman's palaver. And those names, I had heard them somewhere. Could this be...? No, not possible.

My bow crunched on the shelly shore. Just off the little harbor rose the silhouette of a steeple that leaned like that of the Oysterback Hardshell Methodist Church. But Oysterback, town of "three streets at high tide, four at low," a place once described as "over the rainbow and down Tobacco Road," was gone, having disappeared a while back. Even the occasional dispatches and reports that circulated in the big city simply faded away.

It only existed now, I had assumed, in the fevered brain of its creator, Eastern Shore author Helen Chappell, who had been scarce herself of late.

But here it was, improbably, magically, on this foggy, starry night. I was pretty sure when I saw the hand-lettered cardboard notice, on the phone pole next to the church, of "Teen-age Girls in the Old Testament," performed by the students at Patti's Christian School of Tap and Ballet.

And I knew beyond doubt when I rounded the Curl Up 'n' Dye Salon De Beaute, co-owned by Doreen Redmond, wife of Junie, who had been the one back there talking to Hudson (Huddie) Swann, who is Oysterback's resident Vietnam vet and the oysterman who tonged up a mermaid last winter.

And then I was at the place I had longed for all this time—just past the Salon de Beaute and across from Omar Hinton's store—the Blue Crab Tavern.

I entered, and there behind the counter, just back from her annual pilgrimage to Graceland, as I could see from the Build Your Own Elvis Shrine Dashboard Kits she had on special, was the proprietor, Desiree Grinch.

In the dim light, I could have sworn she looked a lot like Helen Chappell. But no, Helen was busy starting a Locally Famous Writers' School up in Talbot County, and prowling Eastern Shore necropolises. Besides, Desiree said tartly, she did not look a thing like Helen Chappell—rather more like Reba McIntyre except more voluptuous, if I were going to describe her.

I said I would need a large-size Wild Goose Ale and some of Desiree's famous oyster pie. I noticed the menu now also featured oyster sushi. Indeed, a lot was changing in Oysterback since the Japanese began buying in, Grinch said.

Hiromoto Lifestyles, the aquaculture and leisure time division of Mitsubishi Corp., has an option on Tubmans Corner from the Boone Bros, whose We Fix & Road Kill Cooked Here Cafe draws the BMW and Volvo set down from Washington for simultaneous auto repairs and fine dining.

Already, a Buddhist temple is going up next to Hardshell Methodist Church. The Boones, if the Japanese deal goes through, plan to go to a-rabbing, they say, hawking "hand-reared oysters" and Ferrus T. Bucket's finely counterfeited decoys to their cosmopolitan clientele.

All the other news of Oysterback came from a table at the Blue Crab, where sat the *Oysterback Bugeye's* editor, Helga Wallop, wife of Poot. A successful artist, Helga's paintings on velvet have been displayed as far away as the First Bank of Delaware. She was joined by the postmistress, Hagar Jump, and assistant deputy sheriff, Johnny Ray Insley.

Oysterback is abuzz over Miss Nettie Leery's subpoena from Ken Starr, who wants to know under what circumstances she visited the Oval Office in 1996. She says everyone knows it was to deliver her Harlequin Pecan Cool Whip Fantasy, with which she has many times won the national Jell-O Mold-off competition held annually in Oysterback. Meanwhile, Huddie and Junie have finished their court-ordered sensitivity training. They will no longer refer to occupants of the Shallow Shoals Doublewide Park as "trailer trash," or to the Washington ladies who have turned the old Grimsby place into a very spiffy B & B as "Martha Stewart Queens."

It has been quite a year for Huddie and Junie. The former completed his degree at Salisbury State's Perdue School of Business, and is offering financial advice to watermen considering raising emus and shedding crabs for the Japanese. The latter is recovered from injuries sustained in a fall from his Gravely while mowing grass and drinking.

Meanwhile still, some things never change. Ferrus T. Bucket, world's oldest waterman and forger of wooden waterfowl, still dreams in perfect Parisian French.

Maybe it was the large Wild Goose, or the fog that crept across the town and seeped through cracks, filling the Blue Crab Tavern, but the next thing I knew I was back in my kayak on a familiar stretch of water where the Transquaking and Chicamacomico rivers flow together. Except for the piquante of "Oysters Desiree" that lingered on my tongue, my visit seemed just a pleasant dream.

Until, that is, I reached into my rucksack and discovered the book you're about to read. How the...? Maybe my dream and the people I met were more fact than fiction. Maybe Desiree Grinch slipped the book into my sack while I threw back my head to drain the last of that beer. Maybe we should try to find Oysterback again, together...

Spring

DOWN TO THE BLUE CRAB TAVERN

A thirty-year-old Cadillac, the worse for wear, original shocking salmon paint faded to pastel peach, bounced across the old wooden bridge over Oysterback Creek and rattled down the road.

It turned into the parking lot of the Blue Crab Tavern, the huge fins seeming to hove about as the brakes squeaked to a stop. A large man in sunglasses and a sagging black jumpsuit emerged and stretched, running his hand over his sideburns, pulling a baseball cap over his thinning gray hair. He looked around at the empty streets, rubbed his aching back and ambled into the Blue Crab Tavern.

The juke was softly playing "A Fool Such as I." An original oil painting of Elvis on black velvet, framed in twinkling lights, hung over the pool table. As his eyes adjusted to the cool darkness, he noted many other relics of The King featured in the decor and shifted uneasily. He was about to turn and run when the aroma of white meatloaf filled his nostrils, drawing him toward the empty counter.

The redhead—Desiree Grinch, proprietor of the Blue Crab Tavern—turned from the Today's Specials chalkboard. "Hey," she said, her smile tainted by a tiny flash of puzzlement, that *I know you but I can't place you* look in her eye. "What can I do you for today?"

"Hey," he returned, squinting at the board hopefully. "Is that white meatloaf?"

"Sure is," the redhead replied. She glanced at the big, Elvis-faced clock on the wall between the bathrooms, doors marked *Sooks* and

Jimmies. "It's almost ready. You're just a shade early for lunch. I generally don't start serving 'til eleven, but I can give you a bowl of cream of crab bacon soup while you're waiting."

Crab bacon soup! He almost licked his chops. "Yes, ma'am, that would be just fine," he replied gravely.

"How about a side of homemade mashed potatoes and some stewed tomatoes with that?" she asked, jotting things down on a pad. "We have three stars from the Guide Michelin, see?" With her pencil she pointed to the chalkboard.

But his eyes weren't on the menu; they were on the deep-dish banana custard pie cooling on the counter. "Why, that's just like my mama used to make," he said. "Back home."

As she ladled the soup into a big bowl, she asked, "Where's home for you?"

"Uh, Memphis," he mumbled. "I mean, Mississippi. Yeah, Mississippi."

"You're a long way from home then. I go to Memphis about once a year to visit Graceland. I guess you can tell, I'm a big Elvis fan," she said, laying down flatware and a place mat that showed you how to pick a crab on the counter. She placed the soup on top.

He ducked his head down close to the bowl, muttering something about having been to Graceland, once upon a time in another life. The soup was delicious, fragrant with crab and bits of bacon floating in a rich, creamy stock.

The oven timer went off. She ducked back into the kitchen, talking as she went. "Yeah, I just love me some Elvis. I don't know what it is about that man, but I just can't resist anything to do with Elvis. You ever see him?"

Happily, she did not wait for a reply, but chattered on about her various trips to the home of the King. The man scraped the last of his soup out of the bottom of the bowl and pulled the bill of his cap further down over his face, a corner of his upper lip quivering as the juke segued into "Are You Lonesome Tonight?" When she emerged from the kitchen bearing a platter of thickly sliced white meatloaf, white gravy, mashed potatoes, and stewed tomatoes, he almost drooled. He had always been able to eat with the best of them.

She gave him that look again. "Would you like something to drink? Beer, coffee?"

"Just an ice tea, please, ma'am," he said. The white meatloaf was, if possible, better than his mama used to make. It melted in his mouth and made him yearn for home. When she laid down a basket of cornbread, it was all he could do not to cry. When she served him a slab of banana cream pie he knew he'd died and gone to heaven.

"I know who you are!" she exclaimed. "You're him!"

"Oh, no! You just think I just look like him," he protested, ready to bolt. After all these years, they still know, he thought.

"You're the new night watchman over to Patamoke Seafood!"

"Yes ma'am, that's what I am!" he said, relieved.

"There!" she exclaimed, grinning. "I knew I'd seen you some-where."

"That must be it," he said, peeling bills off a thick roll.

She shrugged. "Well, it's a small world." He left a generous tip on the counter, took a toothpick from the jar on the register, and head-ed straight out the door.

Just as he opened it, he turned and smiled a familiar, crooked smile. "Thank yew. Thank yew verra much," he said. The screen door swung shut.

It took her several seconds to comprehend, and another second to lunge for the door. She was just in time to see the pink Caddy's tailfins receding into the distance, to hear the old wooden bridge rat-tle as the car crossed the creek and swung into the winding cause-way through the marsh. She stared until the tiny pink blur seemed to gain altitude and rise until it was flying just over the yellow grass, disappearing into the distant place where the marsh and the sky join forever.

DIAGRAMS OF THE MOON

*I*n the full moon, the flowering peach trees look like luminous ghosts. Behind the wheel of her battered van, Duc Tran Swann sits beside the Blue Crab Tavern, surveying the sleeping village by the river. Freshly hatched from a fashionable New York art school, she has a silver stud in her nose and a wild nest of dark hair. Quickly, she shifts into gear and rolls into town, following the map on the dashboard until she comes to the yellow Nanticoke where her father lives. His name is on the mailbox and he is asleep inside, oblivious to the fact he has a daughter he has never seen, doesn't even know he has, with a woman he thinks has been dead since the Fall of Saigon.

Right now, this is what Tran wants.

Quietly, she stops the van and surveys the house in the moonlight. The whole north wall is windowless; this is good. She stares at the blank wall in the moonlight, seeing not vinyl siding, but the vision she has created in her mind.

Quiet as the zephyr in the flowering peach, Tran goes to work. She can only paint by moonlight, she has recently decided. There is a silver quality to the light that enhances her palette of luminous colors. Tran is not given to words; her art says everything she needs to say. Round spheres, whole floating worlds take shape from her quick broad strokes. A blank wall is becoming a work of art. She calls it *Diagrams of the Moon*, pleased with the way in which it is turning out, just the way she saw it in her head. Since she is not a big woman, she has to stand on her ladder to reach the high parts, but the Swanns inside the house—Hudson, Jeanne, and their twin daughters—sleep on, as if under a spell.

Perhaps they are; this is a magic night, when the flowering peach trees bloom and the eels swim into the Devanau River, coming home from the Sargasso Sea, all beneath a silver globe in a starry heaven.

Tran paints on. Like all the young, she believes she will live forever. Like all artists, she believes her work is her immortality. This mural is her message to her father, her way of letting him know she exists. It is a beautiful painting. Even a man whose idea of fine art is a duckscape over the living room couch will see what a great mural Tran is painting; these diagrams of the moon speak to the soul. It is genetically impossible for him not to get the message.

As she paints, she listens to the Lemonheads through her Walkman. When the tape is finished, it turns itself over and plays again.

When she finishes (for now) the false wolf dawn is just peering over the trees on the other side of the river. She stands back to admire her mural. It is good because it says what she wants it to say. She signs it down by the foundation in Viet, using a Magic Marker. She prints the title in English.

Quickly, she caps her cans and folds up her ladder, pushing them into the back of her van. She lets the van roll a little before she starts the engine.

On her way out of town, she sees the kid again, waiting by the softball field at the Blue Crab. He's carrying a nylon backpack and a catcher's mitt, and he looks like he's from Oysterback. She stops for him.

Michael Ruarke climbs into the van. "You do it?" he asks.

Tran nods. "It looks pretty good," she says modestly.

"You think you could pierce my nose like yours?" Michael asks.

"Sure," Tran says. Maybe he's not as big a hick as she first thought when she picked him up coming into town.

"Cool," Michael says. He pushes an MC 900 Foot Jesus tape into the deck.

As the van heads toward Ocean City, Hudson Swann, yawning, comes out of his house on his way to work. As he is getting into his truck, he sees the painting that has appeared on the wall of his house. He studies the moon diagrams and feels something for which he can find no words, only a yearning for something he did not know until now that he has been missing.

IN DRY WEATHER, ALL SIGNS FAIL

W hen you get to a certain age, Miss Nettie Leery thinks, any day you can get out of a chair under your own steam is a good day. But, a day when you find yourself lying flat on your back in the grass in the side yard is something else entirely. She stares up at the sky, achingly blue, framed in the branches of the twisted willow. Somebody tried to tell her it is Harry Lauder's Walking Stick, but she has always known it is twisted willow.

Since it is the corkscrew willow that has landed her in her present predicament, unable to rise, she should blame the shrub, she thinks. Right this minute, she should be attending a flower arranging class, so maybe she should blame all this on Helga Wallop, who is teaching the End of the Line Senior Center ladies a new way to stuff blooms into a block of Oasis. It's something Helga picked up when she and Poot went on that cruise last winter. Miss Nettie privately thinks Helga gets a little silly with her artistic pretensions. But blaming Helga seems silly; she just asked Miss Nettie to bring corkscrew willow to the class today.

But when Miss Nettie went outside to cut some branches from the big bush in the side yard, her arthritis was already giving her trouble. Her knees would barely bend this morning and she had to pull herself out of bed. When she mis-stepped, lost her balance and fell over that cement chicken lawn ornament that has been in the same place for thirty years, she couldn't get up. Still can't get up. Silly, but true.

But miraculously, the pain has abated.

Sooner or later, she knows she'll make a big effort and struggle to her feet, so she's not especially worried. In fact, she's enjoying this unexpected hiatus from her usual activity. If you're Miss Nettie, there aren't enough hours in the day to do everything that needs to be done.

The last time she laid down in this yard, she was a young girl, watching the clouds form and dissolve overhead into fantasy shapes. Could that really have been fifty years ago? It only seems like a short time ago. Pearl, her next oldest sister who used to lie in the grass with her spotting cloud castles and cloud faces, has been dead for seventeen years. She's buried out in Arizona, where she and her husband Walls moved after she had the first heart attack. This reminds Miss Nettie that she should call her other sister Florence, who lives in Wallopsville and sends her Social Security checks to Pat Robertson. Florence hasn't been right since Vietnam.

Miss Nettie has fallen, and she can't get up, just like that silly woman on the TV commercial. The thought makes her chuckle. Usually, her arthritic knees give her plenty of warning before they act up. You can predict the onset of damp weather by Miss Nettie's patellae. But what the old people used to say is true: in dry weather, all signs fail. And it certainly has been dry lately. Those puffy white clouds just drift on by, without a drop of rain falling. And now she's one of the old people. It's true. In dry weather, all signs *do* fail. She's lived long enough to bear witness to that.

Not three feet away, the cat strolls past her with something in its mouth. The mockingbird who lives to torment the ancient tom shrieks angrily from a high branch from the holly tree. It couldn't be a more lovely day, she thinks, for falling and not being able to get up. A faint scent, carried on the breeze, stirs Miss Nettie's memory and she twitches her nose. Vanilla.

I've had the taste of vanilla on my mind for a while now, she thinks. It's like the ghost of a memory of a taste, a yearning for that round sweetness of vanilla. When we went down to the Outdoor Show at Golden Hill at the end of the winter, I bought some vanilla oil from one of the vendors, but it's not the same. You've got to have real vanilla to make a real pound cake.

A ladybug alights on Miss Nettie's arm and she studies it as it studies her. "Ladybug, ladybug," she recites solemnly. "Fly away home. Your house is on fire, your children will burn." The ladybug doesn't seem impressed; it dips its wings and investigates the tiny hairs on her wrist.

Miss Nettie barely notices. She's starting to think about pound cake. There's a half a loaf in the freezer, where she put it down after Easter dinner. And the blackberries are just beginning to come in, down at the edge of the yard where it meets the marsh.

Somewhere inside the house, the phone is ringing. It's her daughter, Miss Nettie thinks. She can almost recognize Jeanne's voice in that angry, insistent ring. Lately, Jeanne has taken it into her head that because her brother Buddy has HIV, he should lie still and quiet in a darkened room, waiting for Death like a gentleman caller. He should wait with his hands folded on his chest and a saintly expression, a Victorian postcard. Instead, Buddy is up in Baltimore having a wonderful time. Whatever they're doing to him at Hopkins, it works; he has taken up acting and appeared on *Homicide* twice. Once as a murder victim, except he was face down on the floor and you couldn't see his face. And the other time, he was one of a group of people in the background when Pembleton was having one of his tantrums. Jeanne thinks that for a man whose death warrant has been signed (her very words) he's having entirely too much fun. As the phone rings and rings, Miss Nettie decides that Jeanne has finally found out that her brother has been cast in John Waters' latest movie. She breathes a sigh of relief when the shrilling stops and the house is quiet again. She won't think about that right now.

Poundcake and blackberries. The taste drifts through her mind, and she can just see it all laid out on the table. With a cup of coffee. There's still some in the pot.

Ultimately, it is pound cake and boredom that force her to slowly and painfully sit up, grabbing the head of the cement chicken, then the low branch of the corkscrew willow to work herself back on her feet again. The knees, for having been so evil only fifteen minutes ago, now seem a little more cooperative. They only shriek a little when Miss Nettie, with a most unladylike grunt, heaves herself to her feet. And they are nice feet, firmly planted on the grass, in their pink Dearfoam slippers. She's grateful to be upright, even if she does feel a little wobbly; this is another small victory against old age.

Miss Nettie picks up her scissors and her corkscrew willow, heading shakily but steadily toward the blackberry patch, the mockingbird and the tomcat following in her wake as if curious to see what will happen next.

COUNT DRACULA HAS A
GOOD HAIR DAY

*A*fter the Ocean City bound Trailways pulled away from Ray Bob's Gas 'n' Go, Count Dracula came out of the men's room and realized that he had missed the bus. When you're a thousand years old, your bladder just doesn't hold up like it did when you were only a kid of five hundred. His suitcase was on that bus, too. Right now it was headed for Thrasher's Boardwalk Fries without him, with the pair of Ward decoys he had just purchased rolled up in his shorts.

"That's too bad," Ray Bob told him. "There's another one tomorrow, though." Ray Bob phoned Ocean City and told them to hold the Count's suitcase down to the depot. He told the Count that he could spend the night at Ye Olde Colonial Watershed Bed and Breakfast over in Oysterback and even gave him a ride in the tow truck, since he was going that way.

"It used to be Ye Olde Colonial Watershed Tourist Home," Ray Bob explained apologetically, "but you gotta change with the times, y'know?"

The Count allowed as how he did know. He was still upset about his suitcase going to Ocean City without him.

Unfortunately, the Ye Olde Colonial was full, since the Swann-Dreedle Family Reunion was that weekend, but Miss Sister Gibbs called Miss Nettie Leery who called Venus Tutweiler, who said that the Count could sleep on the fold-out couch in her TV room at the Shallow Shores Doublewide Park. She assumed that Count Dracula was in town for the family reunion; since he was related to the

Swanns and/or the Dreedles, it was okay that he was a stranger; he knew people she knew. But since Venus had to work a double shift that weekend (they were doing inventory at Patamoke Seafood), the Count would have to get his own breakfast. That was okay with him.

The fold-out had a wafer thin lumpy mattress and one of those bars that rubbed you right across the kidneys, and Venus made up the bed with the Mighty Morphin Power Ranger sheets she uses when her nieces and nephews come to visit. "They're the only ones that fit that fold-out," she told the Count apologetically on her way out the door to work. "Help yourself to anything you find in the fridge."

Unfortunately, he didn't know how to use the microwave, and when he went into the bathroom, everything was so pink and fuzzy and covered with fuschia shag carpet, he was afraid to dry his hands on the towels and wiped them on his morning coat. The potpourri made him sneeze.

So, he took a walk around town.

Down to the harbor, he ran into watermen Junie Redmond and Huddie Swann, who told him quite a lot more than he wanted to know about Maryland politics, the seafood industry, and Rush Limbaugh. Professor Shepherd told him the best place to eat in town was the Blue Crab Tavern, which was where he was headed, if the Count wanted to come along.

The Count, being a stranger in town, stood his new friends some drinks. He had glass of Sangre de Toro himself, but it wasn't what he thought it was going to be. When Desiree Grinch, who runs the Blue Crab, gave him a menu, he sort of shook his head. She asked him if he'd like a nice rare steak, but Count Dracula thought she said "stake," and she had to smooth his feathers down.

It was Huddie who had the bright idea of calling up the Boone Brothers' We Fix & Road Kill Cooked Here Cafe over to Tubman's Corners, and after some telephone conferencing back and forth, Mike Boone brought something over in a biodegradable take out package, which he called Small Mammal Sushi and that seemed to work out pretty well, although no one really wanted to watch the Count eat it.

But he was used to that, and when Doreen came over from the Curl Up 'n' Dye Salon de Beaute to pick up the lunches, he was ready to listen when she said he really, really needed a manicure, and maybe get some of that brillantine out of his hair. A little trim would give him a new touch. "A makeover," she suggested, "would not be inappropriate, Count Dracula, honey."

"And nobody wears white tie before six," Desiree added confidentially to him, patting his hand. "Unless they're being buried."

The Count tried to explain that as one of the un-dead, well, uh, there were certain rules, but Doreen had already dragged him off to the Curl Up 'n' Dye, where Jeanne shook her head over his cuticles, filed his nails, buffed them and applied a coat of clear polish. Fern shampooed him with PH balanced, apple scented stuff that made his nose itch, and gave him advice on which conditioner to use.

Then Doreen plumped him into her station and worked her magic on his hair. He was, she noted, getting a little thin on top, so she layered him up and used just a little Style Hold. He was so pleased with his new look that he tipped generously and bought several salon products unavailable in Transylvania since the break up of the former Soviet Union.

Over to Omar Hinton's Store, Count Dracula bought a Lotto ticket and browsed the rack of camouflage jumpsuits Omar had bought cheap from the flea market to Seaford. He bought one in Deep Jungle. "You never know," he told Omar, who agreed with him completely, especially when the Count told him he was sleeping on the fold-out couch over to Venus's. Omar took pity on him and gave him a toothbrush from stock. He and Thelma slept on that couch during the ice storm last winter, and Thelma's back still wasn't right.

About that time, Ferrus T. Buckett, the world's oldest waterman, wandered into Omar's, looking to cash his Social Security check and buy a fifty-pound bag of Happy Pooch Fortified Dog Food. When he saw Count Dracula, his sharp old eyes, the color of a winter river, lit up. "You look like a man who collects decoys," Ferrus said, licking his chops.

Count Dracula allowed as how yes, he had a modest collection of carved birds, back in his castle in Transylvania.

Ferrus clapped the vampire on the shoulder. "I got one or two 'coys out to my place. Now, I can't guarantee they're real old or nothin', but you ought to come take a look-see, my friend."

Ferrus was still talking as he led him out the door, the Count following him like a fish hooked on a line. "I know a collector when I see one," Ferrus told him. "Now I got a snow goose I just dug out, I mean, found. Could be a Creighton..."

Omar just shook his head. "Poor vampire never had a chance," he sighed.

THE SUBSTANCE OF THINGS NOT SEEN

Chelsea Redmond is thirteen, and in eighth grade this year. Every night after dinner she bikes down to the harbor and baits up her father's trotlines. For this, Junior pays her, and she's saving up the money. Chelsea is the frugal one of the Redmond kids; she lends her brother Jason money at usurious rates of interest. Jason used to bait the lines, but now that he can drive, he's got a part time job over to the Burger Clown in town. The one thing Jason knows is that he doesn't want to be a waterman like his father. He's got some drafting talent, and their mom, Doreen, hopes he'll go to college and become an architect.

No one knows what Chelsea will do; she's quiet and holds her thoughts to herself, like she hoards her money, which she keeps in a Rebman's Chocolate box under a loose floorboard in her bedroom. There's almost four hundred dollars there, Christmases and birthdays and endless miles of salt eel snoods. Getting herself to part with the money to buy the new Smashing Pumpkins CD was a struggle.

But Chelsea has ideas. Last summer, *Pride and Prejudice* was on her reading list, and when she finished that, she went on to *Sense and Sensibility* and then *Northanger Abbey*. Now, she's listening to *Susan* on tape, using her Walkman, a present from her godmother, Desiree Grinch, who runs the Blue Crab Tavern and has been married four times. Desiree has read Jane Austen and understands certain things that Doreen would never in this lifetime understand. Or so her oldest daughter thinks.

While Chelsea baits, holding her breath against the stench of salt eel, and there is no smell quite as bad as salt eel, she wonders what Jane Austen would do if she lived in Oysterback. It's hard to picture Marianne or Elizabeth Bennett baiting up lines. If Jane Austen lived in Oysterback, she would be counting the days until she could leave, move to Manhattan, and get an apartment and a life. Getting a life has been a goal Chelsea has been pondering lately. She knows she needs one, but she's not quite sure how to go about getting it. Chelsea isn't sure what else Jane Austen would do. One thing for sure, there are no Mr. Darcys around here.

Kevin Swann *is* around. Lanky and blond, he's a freshman this year, plays JV football, runs track, so he has to lope around a lot, and he runs around the harbor every evening, in his shorts and West Hundred High School t-shirt. He's known Chelsea all his life, and he's aware that she's down there baiting lines aboard her father's boat, listening to tapes on her headset, but he doesn't think about it too much, except to wonder if she's noticing him since he's started buffing up and got his ear pierced. If he knew for sure that Chelsea noticed him, he might stop and talk to her, or at least make a point of stopping within her line of vision to stretch his hamstrings or something. The very fact that she always seems like she's a thousand miles away in her head intrigues him. Maybe if he got a tattoo she would think he was really cool, but you have to be eighteen or have parental permission, and Miss Catherine and Mister Hardee Swann aren't even worth the asking. They are, of course, hopelessly clueless. Kevin is their youngest, a surprise for their middle years. He gets away with a lot more than his older brothers and sisters, or so they tell him. Kevin doesn't feel like he gets away with much.

Some of the watermen think Chelsea is a real baby doll, but they know better than to try and start anything. Junie Redmond's a watchful father, but Doreen, she'd wipe the floor with some married man and ask questions later, if she felt like it. You'd almost prefer Junie to come after you with those fists of his, the size of footballs, to what Doreen could do to you.

Kevin, however, is not a grubby old waterman of twenty-seven or so with three kids and a resentful, bitter wife, but a teenager who has not yet figured out that he's a hostage to fortune. The world, as far as he is concerned, is his oyster, and the horizons are full of unlimited visibility.

Besides, there's something intriguing to him about a girl doing a boy's job, Chelsea Redmond in her baggy shorts and Spin Doctors t-shirt, hacking apart putrescent chunks of eel, her red hair tucked up under a baseball cap, so that a few strands fall over the back of her neck. It's a very pretty neck, he thinks.

He thinks he would like to touch those strands of coppery hair.

Her mind is two hundred years and five thousand miles away in Regency England, but Kevin doesn't know that. He has only the dimmest idea who Jane Austen is. Ask him anything about the Skins, though.

But he runs down the south leg of the harbor, past the skipjacks all rafted up, comes back and runs down the north leg, so that he passes her twice.

It's getting dark now; the sky over the Devanau River is turning blood orange, and just as he stops, doing a little jogging in place about ten feet away from the *June Debbie's* slip, she looks up.

Kevin and Chelsea make eye contact.

Kevin flushes a deep crimson and takes off at the same time Chelsea drops her gaze to the plastic barrel of salt and eel.

Tomorrow, Kevin thinks as his big ungainly feet hit the asphalt, *I'll talk to her*. He's got twenty four hours to think of something to say.

Chelsea smiles to herself. Jane Austen, she thinks, would be pleased.

The orange sky is a canopy over a new and headlong world of infinite possibility.

☉YSTERBACK ✹ BUGEYE

Helga Wallop, Editor　　　PO Box 3, Oysterback MD 21000　　　25 cents

🦀 *Published every now and then or whenever there's news...* 🦀

Patamoke Patter

The "Patamoke Peeper" has been apprehended by Sheriff Wesley Briscoe. It turned out to be town criminal Alonzo Deaver, who was not peeping, as many have thought, but stealing shrubbery for re-sale to new homeowners at the Shallow Shores Doublewide Park. That's Alonzo's story and he says he's sticking to it.

Paisley Redmond is back at home with wife Beth and son Olivier after his return from an unexpected trip to New York City in the back of the Patamoke Seafood Truck along with a quarter ton of Cap'n Fike's Flash Frozen Breaded Clam Strips. He says from now on he will find another place for nap breaks while working double shifts at the seafood plant, but he enjoyed his visit to Planet Hollywood...

Fribby Dixon reports news from Reverend Claude Crouch, the Traveling Evangelist. Claude, who has been shifting gears for God on the sawdust trail at the True Doctrine Transmission Shop in Virginia Beach, says he is changing lanes once again. Claude says he has received the call to sell time-shares in the new Condos for Christ going up over to Winona...

Mrs. Fenwick Bunting Stockton-Fenwick, a genealogist from Rehobeth Beach who has found a way to trace her lineage back to The Creator, will address the combined Santimoke and Devanau Daughters of Historical Lineage meeting next Tuesday at Mount Boredom, the historical old mansion. Since most of them are of an age to anticipate a meeting with the Great Historical Ancestor in person, this seems appropriate.

Hagar Jump, Oysterback's postmaster, reports that the Patamoke Community Theatre in the Oblong will be offering "Showboat" instead of "Hello Dolly" this spring due to a leak in the plumbing when the pipes burst in the big freeze...

Captain and Mrs. Lennie Skinner are spending a weekend alone at their cottage in Ocean City, where they will be cleaning up for the coming summer renters...

Shelly Briscoe, of Shelly's Buttons 'n' Bows Kountry Krafts will be giving an Easter Bunny Workshop at the Community Center Saturday. Those who wish to make an exciting and unusual Easter Bunny are asked to bring a photograph of Lamar Alexander, a can of stewed tomatoes, and an old tractor-trailer tire...

Bobby Smoot, son of Eulalia Drain Smoot of Wallopsville and Harley Smoot of Patamoke, who has just graduated from Yale *cum laude* last December, has finally found full-time employment after a long search. Bobby will be assuming his duties as assistant second shift manager at the "Buy and Bag" this week. Stop by and wish him well as he hands you your shopping cart...

(See Patamoke p. 2)

(Patamoke from p. 1)

Patamoke Jaycees Pearl "Widge" Tutweiler and Ursus Monie are organizing a bus trip to see all the tourist attractions of Glen Burnie. A box lunch and an English-speaking tour guide will be provided. Anyone who is interested in seeing the sights of this legendary Maryland tourist Mecca should contact Widge down to the office at the Seafood Plant, or Ursus over to Ray Bob's Gas 'n' Go...

Eugene Boudine, musical director of the West Hundred Community Orchestra, will be emceeing the "A Tribute to Seafood Products" Parade celebrating National Manufactured Food Day. The parade will start at the Community Theatre in the Oblong at noon and proceed to the Seafood Plant. Patamoke Fire and Rescue will host neighboring VFD's Oysterback and Wallopsville. The Forklift Precision Drill Team, the West Hundred High School Band, and the All Watermen Elvis Impersonators' Glee Society will also participate. Float themes will include Miss Shrimp Bite, Clam Strips on the March, and Fun with Fish Sticks.

Orville Tutweiler, book critic for *The Bugeye,* will be this month's speaker at Great Books. His topic will be "Testosterone Bridges of Cedar Bend: On Objective Correlative and Negative Capability in the novels of Robert James Waller, Who is Just So Butch."

If Wade and Mookie are out of jail by the opening gun, Mr. Earl's Party Farm will kick off the season with an early bird special Battle of the Bands this Saturday Night. Norris Peavine's Mello-Groov D.J. Services will officiate the non-stop action. Shirts and ties for all the guys, stag and drag admissions. Bands will include Reform School Sluts, Hellbusters, Satan's Hot Dogs, and the Patamoke Community Orchestra's Lush 'n' Easy Strings.

THE D.W. DREEDLE MEMORIAL
TELEPHONE COMPANY

*T*hese days, it's all done by computer from a box in the town office in Wallopsville, but for years, Mrs. Eunice Dreedle ran the telephone company from the back of the funeral parlor. The D.W. Dreedle Memorial Telephone Company is one of those tiny independent companies Bell used to allow to exist so the government couldn't call them a monopoly, which it was anyway. These days, everyone and her brother has got their own phone company, but for a long time, Dreedle was one of a handful.

We didn't get telephone out here 'til after Pearl Harbor. Roosevelt got the power up out here on the WPA, but it was old Doc Dreedle, the undertaker, who set up D.W. Dreedle Memorial Telephone Company in memory of his son.

When their son was shot down by a Japanese sniper on some atoll in the Pacific so small it didn't even have a name, Doc decided he had to do something so Eunice would be able occupy herself. D.W. was their only child, you see.

Eunice was blind. Had been since she was little. Lost her sight in a firecrackler accident one Fourth of July. But it came to Doc to start up the telephone company in their house, which was also the funeral home and make Eunice the switchboard operator. He had the funeral parlor in the front rooms, and she ran the phone company out of the butler's pantry in the back.

Eunice might not have been able to see, but that woman could hear. They say she could hear a bird singing in the marsh grass ten miles away. Musical? That girl could pick up any instrument and play a tune, just like that. But it was her own voice that was her best instrument, a coloratura as smooth as buttercream. She knew all the operas, could sing all those fancy arias. When she launched into "O Patria Mia," the toughest old watermen would get teary-eyed. Miss Eunice could have had a career as an opera singer, if she hadn't married Doc and settled down in the West Hundred.

But she didn't, she married Doc instead. So she sat in the butler's pantry, plugging in those blacksnake lines by touch and feel, saying "number, please" in that musical voice, and ringing down the party lines, connecting us to the outside world with a strand of sound. It was Miss Eunice who got on the line and warned the West Hundred that Hurricane Wanda was heading our way. She could hear the wind changing direction and roaring up the Bay just by the way the phone lines over the marsh clicked and whined, a hollow, echoing sound. People who could see couldn't hear it coming, not the way Miss Eunice could.

The sun was shining and the birds were singing, but that night, Wanda ploughed up the Devanau with a ten foot chop and winds so strong they lifted boats out of the water and houses off their foundations, tossing them around like toys. Floods floated the coffins up from their graves, and set the Leery's chicken house down on the roof of Faraday Hick's tractor shed. That was Hurricane Wanda that Miss Eunice heard coming.

Being as how D.W. Dreedle Memorial Telephone was about half jury-rigged, all held together with electric tape and baling twine, and was down about as often as it was up, people never knew what would happen when they used the telephone. You could ask for Omar Hinton's store, and Miss Eunice would plug you in, but you might end up talking to someone you'd never even heard of all the way up to Tolchester Beach. The party line might give out your ring—two long, one short—and you'd pick it up and find out it was for Little Miss Buck, the church organist down the road. Ferrus T. Buckett would never tell anyone what happened to him, but he ripped the thing out of the wall in 1963 and refused to have another one in his house. But even he didn't blame Miss Eunice. Like the rest of us, she did the best she could with what she had to work with, and with Bosley Grinch and Wilbur Rivers only checking the lines out there during trapping season, what could you expect?

When they found the lump in the back of Doc's neck and sent him up to Hopkins, he wouldn't let Miss Eunice go up with him. Was afraid she'd do herself a hurting, blind as she was, in a strange city with no one to help her. The surgery was touch and go there for a while, and Doc was in the hospital for a good long time after that. The doctors—the real doctors—weren't sure he would make it at first. Doc was in bad shape.

But every night, Eunice would call him up in his hospital room, and sing to him over the phone. You could pick up the headset about nine o'clock at night, when it was real still and quiet, and hear her voice, that beautiful bell canto soprano, singing all his favorite opera songs to him over the party line, like concert.

If you happened to be walking around town at that hour of the night, you could hear her all over town as people picked up their phones just to listen to that beautiful voice singing "Un Bel Di" and a lot of other songs no one knows the name of, but everyone knows the tune to. Old men who couldn't carry a tune in a croaker sack and wouldn't know Puccini from Punch Point would listen in. Little kids would be lulled to sleep on that voice. Tired housewives, sprawled in their chairs of an evening, could feel the weariness rising from them when they heard Miss Eunice sing. Nobody understood the words, but they understood the beauty of that voice.

And as Miss Eunice's voice traveled across the marsh on those lonesome lines, flying through the air all the way up to Baltimore, it must have picked up everyone's good wishes for Doc's speedy recovery and carried them along up to that frightened old man alone and ailing in a strange bed in a city of strangers. Don't you know Doc came home on the ferry the next week?

Well, those fancy doctors up to Hopkins could have called it a miracle if they liked, but what healed old Doc Dreedle was the sound of his wife's clear soprano voice, carried over those old black lines across the marsh and up to Baltimore. All they had was each other, you see, and the sounds of love that bound them together.

EDGAR ALLAN CROW SETS THE RECORD STRAIGHT

Edgar Allan Crow perches uneasily on a crepe myrtle branch. Uneasily because he's too heavy for the delicate twig. Uneasily because crepe myrtle blooms make him sneeze, if the noise coming from his beak could be called a sneeze.

It makes Jeanne Swann laugh.

"You think you're smart, don't you?" he demands. "You try coming back as a crow sometime and see how you like it."

"I'm surprised you didn't come back as a raven," Jeanne says around a mouthful of clothespins. "That at least would have made some sense."

The crow, large and black, feathered with an iridescent green and purple sheen, cocks its head to one side and sneezes again. "No, seriously, lady, I'm trying to tell you something here," he says. "What, do I look like a raven? No way, man! Edgar Allan Crow's the name."

"Be that as it may," Jeanne Swann replies. Almost anyone else who encountered a talking crow while hanging out fine washables on the backyard clothesline would probably run away shrieking or call the *National Inquirer*, but this is Oysterback, where anything can happen and frequently does.

"But you know," Jeanne says, pinning up some pantyhose, "living this far out on the marsh, I'd think...well, never mind." She doesn't want to be rude.

"What?" the crow asks. "What?"

"Well, a talking red-wing blackbird or a talking eagle, maybe...but I don't know. Somehow a talking crow just isn't the same."

"That's exactly what I'm telling you!" Edgar Allan Crow says triumphantly. "My point exactly! We don't get any respect, us crows."

"Then why are you telling me you're the reincarnation of Edgar Allan Poe?" she asks reasonably enough. "I should think you'd want to come back as a raven."

The crow hops to the clothes pole, where he sits, looking dejected. "Stereotyped!" he sqawks. "Believe me, the last thing you want to be is a writer or a crow. No respect either way. Unless you're John Grisham or Big Steve King. Then, hooo boy, bar the door, every idiot with a half-life IQ point thinks you're Great Litter-a-chure. I ask you." The crow laughs bitterly.

Jeanne shakes out a thin cotton blouse, pins it carefully to the line. "I dunno," she says doubtfully. "When the label says DRY

I GET NO RESPECT

CLEAN ONLY, do you wash it out by hand or do you take it to the dry cleaner?"

The crow bends down to peer at the label in the blouse. "Too late now," he says wisely. "You hand washed it already. It's gonna shrink a little now. Anyway, like I was sayin', when I was alive, I couldn't get arrested for awfulness. We starved. Literally starved. Dead? All of a sudden, I'm a genius. Listen, you can have your genius, all I ever wanted was a decent living wage for the work I did. Was that too much to ask? Apparently so. Now that silk jacket, you should never dry clean. Always wash it in mild soap and cold water."

"Thanks," Jeanne says. "So, anyway, you starved."

"And died in a charity hospital raving. And now look, I'm a whole industry. People I wouldn't have given the time of day to when I was alive get six-figure advances for writing what purport to be psychological biographies of my life. Academic nodcocks go around saying they're deconstructing my work. Deconstructing? What the hell does that mean when it's at home? And the movies. Have you ever seen any of the movies that are supposed to be based on my work? If I could, I'd ask for my name to be taken off the credits! No, the last thing you want to be on this planet is a writer! You're the point of an inverted pyramid. Where do all these snobby uptown publishing types think they'd be without writers like me? I'll tell you; nowhere! And yet do we get any respect? Hah!"

"Well, perhaps if you'd finished West Point, gotten a degree and a job," Jeanne comments. "Acted more like a responsible citizen, and less like an artist...."

"Look, lady, I was an artist! I took the risks! I suffered for my art! And what did I get? Ripped off at every turn! And I had some talent! You don't believe me? Ask Shelley! That poor fool didn't have enough sense to hold water in a bucket and he got reincarnated as a flight attendant in Saddle River, New Jersey. I'm not even going to tell you where Louisa May Alcott is, but if you've ever wondered what moron is in charge of programming at CBS, well!"

The crow is really working himself up now; shiny black feathers are flying everywhere, and he's bouncing up and down on top of the clothespole. "I could have been a screenwriter, you know; they offered it to me, but I turned it down. 'Screenwriting is what closes in New Haven on Saturday night' is what I said. Who knew? I could have been in Beverly Hills right now, schmoozing with Sharon Stone, but nooooo! A crow. That was what I chose. A crow!" He shrugs, if a crow can be said to shrug. "Who knew? It sounded good."

"Well, you could have gotten something worse," Jeanne says consolingly. Her mind isn't really on this discussion. When you have to stand on your feet all day doing hair and listening to people spill their anxieties, you learn to tune it all out. Most people, and nearly all writers who have been reincarnated as crows, never notice.

The bird takes a deep breath and calms down a little. "Yeah, I suppose you're right," he says reflectively. "Look at what happened to Charles Dickens. He's a monitor lizard in the Galapagos Islands. Of course, his agent got him on one of those nature documentaries on this Discovery Channel, but Chuck always was a publicity reptile." Edgar Allan Crow chuckles at his own joke.

The carillon down at Oysterback Hardshell Methodist Church peals out the noon hour with the Doxology. "Is it that late?" he asks, and looks at his wing as if expecting to see a watch there. "Look, hon, I'm late. I'm supposed to meet Sinclair Lewis and May Sarton over on a cornfield in Wallopsville like fifteen minutes ago. Not that's that far from here, as the crow flies," he chuckles. "Get it? Get it?"

"Mmmm," Jeanne says around another mouthful of clothespins.

"Anyway, it's been nice chatting with you," the crow says, batting his wings a little. "We'll do lunch soon, okay?"

He doesn't even wait for Jeanne's reply, but sails out across the yard and over the trees, disappearing in three or four strokes of his long black wings.

Jeanne pins some bras and a nightgown on the line. "I've really got to get that dryer fixed soon," she mutters to herself.

A STORY ABOUT SWANN'S ISLAND

Well, I wouldn't say no to one of those beers. Are those roast beef sandwiches? Well, thank you, I *will* have one. No, you don't have to thank me, don't think nothin' of it. I was glad to help out. Always happy to give a tow. If you'd waited till high tide, you might have drifted off, but it felt like your keel was really jammed down into the mud. It's interestin' how many sailboaters run aground on the Swann's Island shoal every summer. Sailboats have too much draft for the shallows around Oysterback. Oughta stay in the channel. Some watermen go aground, too, though of course I never did, bein' from around here. You're just lucky I happened to come past when I did, that's all. If you'd tried to walk that anchor out, you may have fallen into the drop. That's Jack's Hole out there, you know; three hunnert feet deep, they say. But don't feel too bad about runnin' aground. You can't trust the charts around here; the bottom shifts around the island awful fast. You just gotta stay to starboard of the lighthouse and stay in the channel.

Oh, yeah, there *was* an island here, Swann's Island. One of my ancestors used to own it, sometime back there around the Revolution.

It was all of seven hunnert acres then. By the Civil War, it was about four hunnert acres, with farms and churches and stores on it, or so they say. Why, there was even a hotel! I read somewhere that when John Smith and his boys come up the Bay in the 1600s, it was still connected to the mainland. What? Oh, eroded away; washed out bit by bit till there was nothing left but this shoal. I think it was because they logged it off so much, all that oak and poplar and white pine; when all the trees were cut down, there was nothing left to hold the land fast. When I was a kid, we used to go gunning for ducks out here and there was just about ten acres of marsh; an old, falling-down house; and a few old tombstones out here. Even that all washed away in Hurricane Camille. Just the old lighthouse left, over there to mark the entrance to the Devanau River. A drowned land now.

Another beer? Don't mind if I do, if you are. This is a good sandwich. Well, if you can spare another, thank you. Oh, the island's all gone, but they still tell stories about it. Stuff about Blackbeard burying treasure there, and the ghosts of drowned watermen walking the bayshore. But those are all tales. What really happened is more interesting. It's still a mystery.

Oh, yeah, it was back during the first World War, when the hotel was still operating, and the village was a going concern, shipping oysters and ducks up to Baltimore on the steamers. The *Ida*, and I checked and there really was a steamer called the *Ida*, used to put in here in the evening, before she went on up the Devanau and spent the night at Queenspurchase.

Well, the way I heard it, there was a big winter storm that blew ice and snow out of the northeast that lasted two or three days. And the *Ida* was late making Swann's Island; the Bay was starting to freeze up, like it does out here. And when the *Ida* finally got here, there was no one on the dock. So, they sent a crewman off to make her fast. Baskets of oysters and ducks were settin' on the dock, just like they'd been left, but there wasn't a soul around. So, they all come ashore and went on up to the hotel. Not a soul in sight, but the dining room was all set up for dinner, and there was food on the plates, still warm. In the kitchen, the stoves were still going, and the food was bubbling in the pots, pies cooking in the oven, not even burned. But not a soul. So, they went along the main street into the village and it was the same thing. In folks' houses, the lamps were burning and it

was all just like they'd stepped outside for a minute and meant to come right back in. You know, coats on the hook, meals half prepared, beds turned down. But not a living soul, not so much as a cat. It was as if everyone had just left in a terrible hurry. Even the workboats were riding the storm in the harbor, and you'd think if they evacuated the island, they'd have gone in their boats, wouldn't you? No other way off the island. Planes? Well, they had planes in those days, those old biplanes, but you couldn't have gotten a flimsy biplane through that weather.

Nope, everyone just disappeared, and were never heard from again. And don't think people didn't look either; they do say that they spent six months combing the Bay looking for any sign of those folks, maybe fifty or so men, women, and children. It was as if they'd gone up in smoke, just vanished off the face of the earth. No trace of them was ever found.

Well, people sort of avoided Swann's Island after that, they tell me. It got an evil reputation. No one wanted anything to do with the place, and it just sort of fell away. Houses collapsed in on themselves after a while. The old hotel burned in another storm, what was left of it, in the '20s. And the island really started to wash away then. Seemed like every high tide took a little more of it away. Till, like I said, the last of Swann's Island disappeared in Hurricane Camille.

And that's the story. Another beer? No, thank you, two's my limit. I gotta load of crabs I got to get ashore before my buyer gives up on me. Don't like to let 'em rest overnight in this weather. No, no, I was glad to help out. Just stay to starboard of the light and you'll make Queenspurchase Marina before dinnertime; tide's comin' in and you've got some air, so you'll be all right. I doubt your keel's cracked. Sailin's not so bad, once you get the hang of it, which you will one day, you keep it up.

Well, I gotta be on my way now; just throw the line over when I get back on my boat, willya? Oh, you're welcome! And you have a nice day, too!

What? What? I can't hear you over my engine! What do *I* think happened to those people on Swann's Island? I don't know! But some folks around Oysterback think they were all kidnapped by aliens and taken to Uranus. Of course, some people will believe *anything*!

☉YSTERBACK BUGEYE

Helga Wallop, Editor   PO Box 3, Oysterback MD 21000   25 cents

🦀 Published every now and then or whenever there's news... 🦀

God Is a Jell-O Mold

If God is in the details, then He was certainly in the Devanau County Jell-O Mold Contest at the Wallopsville Volunteer Fire Company last Saturday. Not a detail was spared as Oysterback's very own Mrs. Antoinette "Nettie" Leery came down to the finals with Patamoke Champion Mrs. Louisa (Sister) Gibbs for the coveted Title of "Jell-O Mold Maker of the Year."

Judges were hard pressed to chose between Nettie's Harlequin Fantasy Delight, whose ingredients included walnuts, cream cheese, Cool Whip, and Mandarin oranges in an alternately layered base of Black Cherry and Key Lime, and Sister's Praline Surprise, which used pecans, Miracle Whip, fruit cocktail, and miniature marshmallows in a special blend of Strawberry Surprise and Banana Delite.

Judges included Patamoke Fire Chief Aldredd (Sheppy) Rackham; Ms. Viola Durkee, Dietary Supervisor of Memorial Methodist Hospital; Wanda Wingo, Devanau County Extension Agent; and Mr. Narthax Tutweiler, head of Food Services at Devanau County Consolidated High School. You can be sure that all the judges are experts in Jell-O, and were hard pressed to make a decision.

After several taste testings, Nettie Leery was proclaimed the winner. Her recipe will be published in a future issue of *The Bugeye*, and she plans to spend the winner's weekend in Ocean City at Lennie and Fern Skinner's rental cottage with her close friend Captain Elmo Rainbird, the retired skipjack owner.

Needless to say, folks down here below the Mason Dixon line take their Jell-O Molds very seriously, and Nettie will be competing in the Regional Jell-O Mold-Off in Baltimore next month. Good luck, Nettie!

And special praise to Sister Gibbs for being such a good sport. You just can't keep those Patamoke women down. Sister promises she has a brand new entry for the Mosquito Festival Velveeta Bake-Off next month. Sister says it's a killer.

• • •

We were all very excited and happy for Hudson Swann and Duc Tran, the daughter he didn't know he had from Vietnam when they were reunited recently at a cookout at the Blue Crab Tavern. Desiree took videos of the event, and Jeanne Swann made a sheet cake to celebrate the happy event with Huddie, Jeanne, Duc Tran, and the twins Amber and Ashley very tastefully portrayed in the icing.

For those of you who have been on Uranus, Duc is the one who painted that great mural of Elvis Ascending a Staircase on the west wall of the Blue Crab. A recent School of Visual Arts graduate from New York City, she is accepting mural commissions for houses, businesses, and workboats. She will

(See God p. 2)

(God from p. 1)

also be playing shortstop for the Jimmies this summer, replacing Alzono Deaver, who has been dismissed from the team after that incident with the stolen bases. Welcome to Oysterback, Duc Tran Swann!

• • •

In Post Office news, Hagar Jump wants everyone to know that the *Waterman's Gazette* and everyone's post-cards from Omar and Isobel Hinton's vacation to West Virginia are in and have been gotten up. Sounds like Omar and Isobel are having a good time going to the flea markets and auctions and visiting the grandchildren. Incidentally, Ray Bob Whortley, and Bubba Clash, your box rents are due.

Beth and Paisley Redmond report that they saw Chessie off Log Cabin Point last Sunday. He says to say hello to everyone down to the Blue Crab, Beth says. Just kidding, aren't you, Beth? (Ha ha!)

• • •

Professor Shepherd, who lives on his boat in the harbor since he lost his tenure at the college, has finally found a new job as a clam checker for the DNR. He says the best thing about his new job is there's no commute, since he can just roll out of his bunk and be at work. He can still give out grades, so all you clammers be good and keep those manoes iced down to 60 degrees or less for the prof, you hear?

• • •

Murilla Meekins and Sudie Fairbank presented a Ree-Veel Christian Bridal Lingerie Shower over to the Blue Crab in honor of their cousin Wytnee Watkins. Wytnee received many fine pieces of Ree-Veel Christian Lingerie from her family, friends and co-workers at the View 'n' Chew Video and Sub Shop. All the ladies enjoyed the artistic dance performance of entertainer Stud Hunk, The Missionary Man. Desiree Grinch reports he definitely gave her an epiphany.

• • •

Parsons Dreedle over to Dreedle's Funeral Home and Country Produce, reports a special offer this week. For every funeral, the bereaved family will receive a bushel of homegrown Big Beef tomatoes and a jar of West Hundred Marsh Mallow honey. Things must be slow over there.

• • •

All the action was over to Patamoke last weekend when Mr. Earl's Party Farm presented a Rush Limbaugh wet t-shirt lookalike contest. Dittoheads from all over the tri-state region came to share their phobias on almost every subject. Winner of the contest was Boo Boo Dyott whose first prize was a trip to New Jersey, where he will have lunch with the Cherry Hill Serial Killer. Boo Boo's wife Illona is filing for divorce.

LITEY CLASH COMES TO PAY UP

I was up on the counter chalking up the White Meatloaf Special on the blackboard the other day when I heard the clang of fifteen pounds of gold jewelry and Litey Clash walked in.

Now, no matter what people may say, I Desiree Grinch, proprietor of the Blue Crab Tavern (★★★ *Guide Michelin*) have nothing against Litey, or that watering hole he chairs down in Wingo, Virginia, the Dew Drop Inn. If someone wants a crabcake about the size of a baby's fist deep fried in a hogshead of grease and served with a side of vegetables boiled until they're olive drab, I almost always recommend the Dew Drop.

Still and all, I was pretty surprised to see him in Oysterback after the Dew Drop softball team, the Lounge Lizards, lost the playoffs to our Blue Crab Jimmies again this season. My questions were quickly resolved when I saw he was carrying a case of Accomac Merlot, the *vin du pays* of his neck of the woods, and a fine *vin* it is, too.

"Well, I am here to pay up, Desiree, and never let it be said that a Clash welshed on his bets," says Litey as he sets the case on my clean bartop. "But next year, we'll hammer you. Snake Wingate will be out of jail by then."

I looked at his matching diamond pinkie rings. "Have you been hitting Burt Reynolds's yard sales again?" I asked him as I got down two glasses and the corkscrew. I selected a bottle from the case and drew the cork. Accomac Merlot doesn't breathe—it gasps for air, so I had time to set out a plate of melba toast and Gostjetöst.

Unfortunately, this also gave Litey time to develop a suitable rejoiner.

"Pretty good for someone who's pulling thirty on a boat hitch," he says.

"They say that if you ever fell overboard, you'd sink right to the bottom, weighed down by all that gold." I poured just a little wine into one glass; it had nice legs. I enjoyed the way that faint, fruity tang rolled on the back of my tongue—the sign of a good, rich Accomac table wine. "'93 was a bad year for Wingo ball players, but a good year for Wingo wine," I remarked.

"Nice talk from someone from Oysterback! This place is so small, you have to rent a town drunk." Litey says, tasting his wine. He closed his eyes and savored it, the only thing to do with a good Accomac Merlot.

"At least our family trees have forks," I replied.

"You call Oysterback a town? Three streets at low tide and two at high," Litey says.

"If I owned hell and Wingo, I'd rent out Wingo and live in hell," I replied. I brought out a slice of green-peppercorn-paté-Desiree and a couple of tart Northern Spy apples. Litey cut the Northern Spies into paper-thin slices and I spread the brie on some sesame biscuits. It was soft and runny, just perfect.

"I'd sooner live in Wingo than Oysterback. People up here are so backward the Episcopalians are snake handlers," he remarked. I filled up both wine glasses again.

"Well, the only thing you need to be a socialite in Wingo is a working set of jumper cables," I observed.

Litey tried another piece of goat cheese and nodded. "I hear things on Oysterback are so dull that a bug zapper is considered quality entertainment."

"Down to Wingo, a seven course meal is a six-pack and a crab-cake," I sighed. If you wait, after a while, you can just taste the ocean wind in the bouquet of Accomac Merlot. Maybe it's because the vineyard is within a mile of the Atlantic.

Litey poured out the last of the bottle into our two glasses. We both savored it.

"Well," I said when Litey got up to go, "at least we don't live in Church Hill."

He shuddered so hard all his chains clanged at once. He sounded like Marley's ghost. "There's a thought," he said.

I waited until he was out the door and into his Cadillac. "The favorite car color in Wingo is primer!" I called out the door.

I like to have the last word.

ALONZO DEAVER GOES STRAIGHT

*T*he one thing that used to be certain in Oysterback, aside from death and taxes, was that if a theft had been committed, Alonzo Deaver was the culprit. The Deaver clan has always been a bit shaky on the concept of other people's personal property, but Alonzo is so bad at it that he always gets caught. But, now that he is out of the Detention Center following that Shallow Shores Doublewide Park shrubbery stealing incident, Alonzo has sworn that his sordid criminal past is behind him and from now on, his yard care business is strictly legitimate. But, if it weren't for a timely intercession from the Boone Bros, Alonzo might have continued his life of crime.

It was early November, and Gabe and Mike were paddling their canoe along the shoreline of Razor Strap Creek in search of the evening's entrée (you don't want to know) at the Boone Bros We Fix & Road Kill Cooked Here Cafe, when they heard yelling over at Colonel and Mrs. Mad Dog Tutweiler's.

Since Gabe and Mike came in off Uranusville Marsh, where they've been living off the land since 1968, to rejoin civilization, they've gotten a reputation around these parts for fixing things. So, they tie up their canoe to the Tutweiler's osprey platform and wade ashore. Mad Dog, Maisie, and Alonzo were all standing around the pool, which is on the creekside, and Mad Dog and Alonzo were engaged in heated debate.

"If Ida known last March that you was a crook, I never woulda hired you to take care a my yard!" Mad Dog is yelling, all red in the face.

"I was a crook last March, but I never stole no pearl necklace! I'd never steal nothing so sissy!" Alonzo replies, deeply insulted.

"Now, boys," Maisie says, but they aren't listening to her. She sees the Boone Bros and waves them in to mediate.

Seems like last spring, before the Tutweilers went to Maine, they hired Alonzo to do some garden work for them. They retired here, so they don't know his reputation. Now, Maisie Tutweiler had a pearl necklace—real pearls, not cultured—that belonged to her grandmother and she wore them almost all the time, even when they were taking up the last of the daffodils around the pool, while Alonzo was over on the other side of the house turning up the garden.

It was a warm day, so when they finished, Maisie and Mad Dog decided to take a swim in the pool. Maisie took off her watch, her gardening gloves, and her pearls, laying them on the bench while she went in the house to change into her swimsuit and turn on the pool heater. The Tutweilers are in the house about a half hour, they tell Mike and Gabe. When they come out, the watch and the gloves are still on the bench, but the pearls are gone. No one else could have come or gone from the road; the Tutweilers would have seen them. No one could have come by because the ospreys were nesting on the platform in the creek, and if a boat had come near, those old fish hawks would have set up a big fuss. Still, the pearls are gone. Vanished into thin air.

"Or into Alonzo's pocket," Mad Dog growls, "and if I'd known he was a thief, I woulda called the police then and there," which sets Alonzo off again, saying maybe Mad Dog took 'em for the insurance money like this *Rockford Files* he saw in jail.

While they are feathering up on each other, Mike and Gabe look around, all around. They don't say anything, at least nothing that anyone else can hear. Finally, they nod to each other and head for the Tutweiler's garage, where they pull out a ladder and carry it down to the creek, wading in about waist deep, until they get out to the osprey platform, about twenty feet offshore from the pool. The ospreys are all gone south by now, so there's nothing left but their big

old lair up there on the piling. And while Gabe holds the ladder steady in the muddy creek bottom, Mike shimmies on up into the nest.

Of course Alonzo and the Tutweilers have stopped arguing to watch this. They're convinced the Boone Bros, who most people think are a slice of cheese short of a reality sandwich anyway, have really fallen off the lunch counter this time.

Mike's up there, legs dangling out of the nest, which is about as big as he is, tossing out twigs, mud, fish hawk dung, bones, rope, crabshells, a man's shirt, shredded inner tube, all the scavenged plunder that fish hawks use to make their flimsy aeries. Of course, the Boone Bros know all about fish hawks, having lived with them in Uranusville Marsh.

Suddenly, Mike gives a whoop and holds up a matinee length string of beads coated in dried-up osprey poop and feathers.

"My pearls!" Maisie cries, because she'd know them anywhere.

"Them ospreys is like magpies and pack rats. They're great ones for pickin' up bright objects when they're nesting," Gabe points out after he and Mike have waded in and picked most of the feathers and osprey guano off themselves. "While you was in the house, they must have cruised them pearls and decided they was the perfect grout for the south wall. Just swooped right down, grabbed 'em up in them great big talons, and carried 'em off. Wouldn't take but a second. Them fish hawks is fast bunkies."

"It was almost the perfect crime," Mike added.

Anyway, now Alonzo Deaver says he's swearing off a life of crime. He says it's no fun when even a fish hawk is smarter than him.

LOVE FINDS PROFESSOR SHEPHERD

It's a sign of spring, when the tourists start coming around Oysterback with their cameras and their yearning for the missing pieces in their lives. It's a rare weekend when you don't encounter a plague of bicyclists spread all over the causeway swatting mosquitoes and deer flies. Mommies and daddies with their tired-out children are buying ice cream over to Omar Hinton's store, looking for a bathroom. Sometimes you have to wonder why they come here; it's not like we're picturesque or anything. The fanciest store around here is Pink's Bait Boutique over to Patamoke, and our only museum is the glass case of pottery shards in the town hall from when they tore down the old brewery after Hurricane Wanda. After you've been to the harbor to look at the workboats you've pretty much done the tour. Most of our visitors are too unsophisticated to understand the subtleties of Desiree Grinch's cooking at the Blue Crab Tavern (★★★ *Guide Michelin*), and too smart to sample the cuisine at the Boone Bros We Fix & Road Kill Cooked Here Cafe and Garage.

Professor Shepherd says that most of us are only a generation or two removed from the farm and the small town, and there's some sort of genetic longing, some ancestral impulse to return to places like the places where our ancestors lived. Suburbia, he says, is an unnatural condition. Well, you'd have to talk to him about it, he's got quite some theories, but I guess I've laid out the essentials.

The professor's had us under the microscope since he didn't get tenure over to the college and started to live on his boat down to the harbor. He works part time at the Blue Crab, checks clams for the DNR, and follows the stories on TV, but he's been working for years on a book about the West Hundred that he says will explain the entire cosmos when finished. Something about us being the microcosm that defines the macrocosm, I don't know. Remember, this man named his boat *Moral Ambiguity*.

Now, when you think of love and romance, Professor Shepherd is about the last person you'd expect to see hit by Cupid's arrow. One of those Medieval hermits who lived on top of a pole had a better chance of meeting Ms. Right. But this is Oysterback, where anything can happen and frequently does.

One fine Saturday, when the sun was shining and the tourists were flocking like grackles around the harbor, their voices warbling *grack, grack, grack*, Professor Shepherd was sanding down his brightwork and reading Hannah Arendt. Love was the last thing he was expecting.

He didn't hear the squeak of her bicycle as she stopped on the gravel not six feet away from him, nor feel her eyes studying him behind her sunglasses, or see the smile that illuminated her face as she scanned the title of his book.

"The banality of evil!" she exclaimed.

Well, that comment made Professor Shepherd look up, you can bet. People in Oysterback don't think evil is banal at all; the time the devil himself had to come and fetch Haney Sparks back to hell after he went AWOL convinced most people evil was at least interesting.

"Carla!" Professor Shepherd cried in instant recognition. "But, but...you're being held prisoner by Stud in the secret mountain stronghold under his log cabin until he can get Victoria to sign the adoption papers!"

"I'm Bambi Bayard, the actress who plays that scheming Carla Devane on *Hapless Hearts*, your favorite daytime drama," she said. "And I hope you are Professor Shepherd, because that is who I am looking for here."

The professor felt, of course, like a complete fool. He knew it was just a story and she was an actress. It was just that seeing her in the harbor in full biking gear was the last thing he expected, even though he had sent her a fan letter.

"You see," the actress continued, "you put your monograph for the *Quarterly Journal of Esoteric Literature* into the envelope you addressed to the show. Before the editors got it straightened out, I'd read your work, and I must say that I was impressed." She smiled, the dazzling smile that made strong soap men bend to Carla's will. "You see, most people know I have a degree in drama, but the *Hapless Hearts* producers try to keep my minor in literature a dark secret. Carla, as you know, can barely read the pictures in *People* without moving her lips."

"Literature?" Professor Shepherd repeated. He sounded stupid even to himself. It's not every day the goddess of your dreams rolls into Oysterback.

"I thought your take on narcissism and the secondary characters in the works of Maria Gaskell was brilliant. And then, when I finally got the letter you wrote, I knew I wanted to meet you. So," she shrugged lightly, "when the writers stashed Carla in Stud's mountain stronghold, I took off on a Shore Tour, hoping to meet you. And here I am." Bambi gestured around the harbor, her inch long eyelashes fluttering. "I'm staying at the Ye Olde Colonial Watershed B and B."

All Professor Shepherd could do was open and close his mouth. For once in his life, he was nonplussed.

But that didn't bother Bambi Bayard. "I don't suppose you know where a girl can get a good crabcake and a discussion about the role of the clergy in the novels of Jane Austen around here, do you?" she asked hopefully.

Professor Shepherd swallowed hard. "As I matter of fact, I do," he said, offering her his arm.

Summer

WELCOME TO
OYSTERBACK

POP: 687

THE BOONE BROS WE FIX & ROAD KILL
COOKED HERE CAFE

I tell you, sometimes it's awfully hard to be the voice of sanity in an open-air insane asylum like Oysterback.

I'm not worried about competition from the Boone Bros' new business. Would you worry about a place with a sign out front that says "Boone Bros We Fix & Road Kill Cooked Here Cafe?" I, Desiree Grinch, proprietor of the Blue Crab Tavern (★★★ *Guide Michelin*) think not.

Ever since Mike and Gabe Boone reappeared from Uranusville Marsh after going underground or somewhere in 1969, they have managed to keep themselves real busy with that old junkyard and trash emporium they opened up over to the old Esso station at Tubman's Corners. If your '78 Pacer blows a rod or you're in search of a box of mayonnaise jars for your tomato canning, you go see the Boone Bros. But I love to listen to Gabe play that trumpet, all those old riffs blowing out across the fields and the river, floating off into the woods like shards of forgotten ghosts.

Doreen, who, as you know, runs Doreen's Curl Up 'n' Dye Salon de Beaute, says they're kind of like scavenger beetles and serve a valuable function in the post-consumer junk chain, since everything the Goodwill won't even think about taking ends up at their place.

But you really have to think twice about going over there to eat dinner with them, as I found out the other day. People who eat out of their traps are one thing; people who eat road kill just aren't to be trusted to work within the recognized gastronomic framework, if you know what I mean and I think you do. Preparing game you've trapped or shot is one thing (and I think I do a mighty nice apple wood smoked Canada goose, myself), but eating an animal that has met an untimely end on Route 50 under the wheels of a Chinaberry Poultry Farms eighteen-wheeler is a might more chancy, especially in warm weather.

For people who have been out of the world for almost twenty-five years, it seems like the Boone Bros are learning the ways of the '90s real fast. The minute they found out what yuppies are, and that yuppies will do *anything* as long as someone says it's trendy, they introduced their road kill menu to an unsuspecting world, and on the weekend you will see all the trend-sucking dilettantes and their BMWs and Miatas lined up three deep around that old garage, sampling Gabe and Mike's blacksnake stew and near-deer pie.

Hagar Jump, who would know, says she saw Madonna and her entourage around there last week, sucking up sweet and sour toad-fish and atmosphere. I say Madonna is so passé she'd go to the opening of a door to get publicity.

Now everyone over to Tubman's Corners is real upset, because it's been peaceful around there since the cops busted that chop shop that used to be in the old Esso. Everyone thinks they're in an episode of the *Beverly Hillbillies* or something. But then, those are the same people who think Eastern Shore folk say "arsters" for "oysters," and I'll tell you: I have never heard an Eastern Shore native say "arsters," just the foreigners. If you get my drift.

Anyway, now the boys tell me they are working up the *Boone Bros We Fix & Road Kill Cooked Here Cafe Cookbook.*

"I hope we can get it done before we have to discorporate and go back to Uranus," Gabe told me the other day.

"Yeah," Mike says. "We have to get a load of crabcakes up to the Mother Planet. We're due for our ten-thousand-light-year oil change on the truck."

Helga Wallop, who edits *The Bugeye*, knows a good thing when she sees it. She's photocopying the cookbook for them at twenty-five

cents a page. She says the Small Mammal Divan recipe isn't half bad, but you ought to stay away from the Cooper's Hawk Paté.

I'm not calling the health department. I'll put that cookbook right up on the counter for sale. This is too interesting to fool with. Every once in a while, you catch a train that you've just got to ride to the end of the line, just to see where it stops. Nature's just got to take its course, but I want the make and tag number of anything I eat over there.

P.S. I wouldn't touch the field greens, if I were you.

SIX DEGREES OF
CORNBREAD MUFFIN

I t's amazing how these things get started.

I, Desiree Grinch, proprietor of the Blue Crab Tavern, am all for a little excitement, but this muffin thing got way out of hand, and frankly, I am glad that what happened, happened when it did.

It was early on a Friday, at lunchtime, when it started. Beth and I had been making cornbread muffins that morning. I don't know about you, but I think there's nothing quite like cornbread muffins when you're serving kale-stuffed ham, which was the special last week, in case you were out of town and missed it.

"Desiree, come look at this," Beth says to me, and like a fool I went over and took a look. Hindsight being 20/20 like it is, I probably should have told her I was busy, but I didn't. She was holding up this muffin that had just come out of the oven, and she says, "What does that look like to you?"

"A cornbread muffin," I said, then I looked closer at the ridges and swirls, the golden brown nooks and crannies. It was one of nature's jokes; they came together and formed a face.

"Wow, is that...?" I asked.

"Newt Gingrich!" Beth crowed triumphantly.

Well, somehow or another, the way the cornbread batter baked, you know the top of that muffin did look awfully much like Newtie. Or somebody. There was a face in there all right.

"Look, it's got them little chubby cheeks and that scowl and them shifty little pig eyes and everything," said Junior Redmond, who'd come around into the kitchen to see what the fuss was all about. "Ain't that just about cute?" He went to poke it with one of those big old fingers of his and Beth snatched it away from him.

"It look just like Bill Clinton to me," he mumbled defensively.

Well, I looked at it again, and it did look like Bill Clinton if you looked at it one way, but then, it looked like Newt Gingrich if you looked at it from another angle. But then again, I have privately thought Clinton and Gingrich always looked as if they were separated at birth, or sporing, or whatever creates politicians.

"Don't you ruin this, Junie," Beth said, snatching the anthropomorphic baked good away from her brother-in-law. "This muffin is a sign from God!"

Well, I cannot say that a face on a muffin is a sign from God, but Beth, who has been broody lately, took that muffin and put it under a glass pastry dome up on the counter. She hand lettered a sign that said "See The Celebrity Muffin" and stuck it on top.

Faraday Hicks, who happened to be sitting next to it, eating a hot turkey sandwich, called to Ferrus T. Buckett and Omar Hinton down the counter. "See that there face in the muffin?" he asked with his mouth full. "Don't that look just like Syndey Greenstreet?"

Ferrus peered at the muffin nearsighted-like. "Naw, it don't look nothin' like Syndey Greenstreet. It does look just like Brady Anderson, though."

"Kyle Secor," offered Hudson Swann, who had just wandered in looking for change for the phone. He got right up on top of the glass dome and squinted hard. "Yes, I'd have to say that muffin looks just like that there actor Kyle Secor. It's got his big ole nose and everythin'."

"Desiree!" exclaims Mrs. Carlotta Hackett. "You've got a celebrity muffin there that looks like Anais Nin. Can I have two cheeseburgers and an order of cole slaw to go?" They're reading diarists at Great Books again, I thought, but that was about all I had time to think, because the lunch rush was pouring through the door like a herd of stampeding buffalo. I don't know what it is about Fridays, but there's something in the air that makes everyone in the known universe want to eat lunch out that day.

Omar Hinton, who is really tall, didn't have to push his way past the lunch crowd at the counter to get his look at the muffin. He just peered down over Miss Carlotta's great big blond bouffant. "I'll tell you what that muffin looks like, it looks like E. Power Biggs."

"Celebrity muffin? Lemme see?" said Parsons Dreedle, who's not so tall and snuck in under Huddie's armpit. "It looks like somebody all right, but I can't...move, Ferrus, I want to see, too. Well, I'm damned! That muffin is the spitting image of Reba Macintyre! Lookit...."

Before I could stop them, they were all crowding around the counter, almost crawling one on top of another trying to get a look at the physiognomic muffin.

"Dennis Rodman!"

"Hannah Arendt!"

"Roger Tory Peterson!"

"Eunice Shriver!"

"Pope Leo VI!"

"Diane Rehm!"

"Mike Ditka!"

"Sherlock Holmes!"

"Joan Baez!"

"John..."

There was a clatter as they swept salt shakers and silverware off the formica in their haste to identify a famous face in a baked good. Small town, not much to do, but still and all, by noon, the next day, it was looking like a mini-riot in here, and someone had alerted the media, so that there was a couple of satellite trucks outside and about eleventy-seven people inside and more coming. This place can only legally hold about fifty, and there must have been about a hundred West Hundred fools crammed into this place, all of them dying to get a look at the cosmic muffin.

"Edgar Allan Poe!" said a tourist as he knocked my twelve point buck off the wall trying to get a picture. Everyone agreed it looked like someone; it was just that no one could agree on exactly who.

"I've been waiting here an hour to get my lunch and I've had just about enough!" Junior Redmond cried, shouldering his way through the crowd. And when Junie shoulders, you can believe he shoulders; he used to be a line backer in high school. He parted that crowd like Cecil B. DeMille parting the Red Sea, and made his way toward the counter. With a roar, he picked up the dome on one hand and the muffin in the other.

He held that muffin over his head as if he were displaying a precious jewel, then slowly, slowly lowered that cornbread to his giant open mouth. It looked like a pat of butter going into a cave.

As he swallowed it, in one enormous bite, there was a collective sigh from the crowd, as if a spell had been broken. In twos and threes, people began to drift away. The camera men turned off their lights, and the tourists shrugged, mumbling, looking for the bathrooms. It was like someone had pulled the plug, the way people drained out of the place.

Junie chewed, swallowed, then looked at me. "Now," he said plaintively, "can I *please* get me some lunch?"

OYSTERBACK 🦀 BUGEYE

| Helga Wallop, Editor | PO Box 3, Oysterback MD 21000 | 25 cents |

🦀 *Published every now and then or whenever there's news...* 🦀

THE BOONE BROS WE FIX & ADVICE TO THE LOVELORN

Dear Boone Brothers:

I hope you guys can help me. My new boyfriend is good at two things and one of them is being a rebel who lives by his own rules, so maybe you can guess what the other one is.

My family and friends say to break up with "Mookie" because he has no job, no car, three kids by four different women, a nasty ex-wife who's suing him for back child support and alimony, a rap sheet (it wasn't really, *really* his fault, and besides, it's on the stet docket), and is also really crazy and undependable and couldn't tell the truth if you held a shotgun to his head and he never calls or takes me out anywhere.

But I love "Mookie" because he is really good looking and has this gorgeous red hair and a buffed bod that makes all the other women wild. And I know he loves me, because he left his rollerblades at my house. Now I think he might be seeing someone else behind my back and I am frantic.

What should I do? I'm desperate.

-Panicked in Patamoke

Dear Panicked:

"Mookie" sounds like he has all the qualities that women really fall for, no matter what they say about nice, sensitive guys who sit on the edge of the bed and say they can't see you the same day they go beat drums at their men's group.

However, you don't mention that criti-cal substance abuse problem that a really desirable guy would have, so I'd think twice about him. -Gabe

Don't get any "Mookie" tattoos. -Mike

Dear Boone Brothers:

I really enjoyed your sun-dried jelly-fish in rosemary sauce special last Tuesday. Will you run it again soon?

-Wallopsville Gourmet

Dear Gourmet:

That recipe and many others are avail-able in our new "Boone Bros We Fix & Roadkill Cooked Here Cafe Cookbook," available at many fine stores and gas sta-tions in the local area. -Gabe

You'll want to check out our Tuesday nite special this week, too. Bear paws and chicken necks à la Catonsville and a tire rotation. A real taste treat for you and your car or truck! -Mike

Dear Gabe and Mike,

I am really in a whole world of confu-sion and I hope you can help me with this one. A while back, my live box was stolen down to the harbor, and I lost about 400 lbs of eels. Recently, I noticed that my best friend had acquired a new live box, but it looks a lot like my old

(See Advice p. 2)

(Advice from p. 1)

live box. I don't want to accuse him of stealing my live box, but the suspicion is driving me crazy. Also, I want those 400 lbs of eel back. I don't care about my wife, he can keep her, but that was a good live box.

-Self-Employed Waterman

Dear Self:

Maybe he liked your live box so much he made himself one just like it. -Gabe

I know your wife. I'd steal the live box back. -Mike

Gentlemen;

What is the meaning of life? I need to know this for a school report.

-Devanau Comm. College Student

Dear Student:

Fixing things. -Gabe

That's what's wrong with this MTV X-Generation: a nine-second concentration span composed mostly of vicarious violent experiences and mosh pits. Take two peyote buttons, listen to "Dark Side of the Moon" all the way through three times, and call me in the morning. I've got a line on some Dead tickets. -Mike

Dear Gabe 'n' Mike,

What is the capitol of Georgia ?

-Curious on Black Dog Road

Dear Cure:

Mylanta. -Gabe

Better yet, have you ever wondered if

New Jersey exists just to keep a safe distance between us and New York? -Mike

Dear Gabe and Mike:

My daughter is getting married in the fall and she is driving me crazy. She has decided that she and all her bridesmaids will wear black. In my day, black was for funerals and cocktail parties, not weddings. What is the correct etiquette these days?

-Mother of the Post-Modern Bride

Dear Bridal Mom:

If the wedding's after six, and the reception is in the Graceland Tiki Room at the Colonial Tropicana Versailles Reception Palace, basic black with pearls is always correct. It compliments the ice sculptures. Black tie or dark suits for the gentlemen, please! If you really want to enrage her (and you probably will, before this is all over) wear bright red. -Gabe

Either she's engaged to Count Dracula or she's going into deep mourning over having to start her married life in a garage apartment behind her in-laws' chicken houses. -Mike

Dear Boone Bros;

Have you ever actually seen a baby seagull? A seagull egg? Did you ever stop to wonder if those big seagulls you see flying around are actually baby seagulls and they grow up and become the size of a Tilt-A-Whirl? And if they do, where are they, somewhere way out to sea? And what will we do of they all decide to attack us one day at the beach in

(See Advice p. 3)

(Advice from p. 2)

Ocean City? I like really need a reply soon.

　　　　　　　　　　　　　-OC Surfer Dude

Dear Dude:

Hope they head for the boardwalk and attack couples from Glen Burnie wearing matching obscene slogan t-shirts. -Mike

How did you figure out our dark secret? Now we'll have to silence you forever by taking you on a permanent vacation to the Uranus. pipleline, heh, heh. -Gabe

Got a problem? Feeling incorrect? Need an answer? Any answer? Address the Boone Bros We Fix c/o this newspaper. Sorry, Gabe and Mike's busy career as untrained (but perfectly legal under Maryland law) counselors allows no time for personal replies, but if you drop over to Tubman's Corners and they're not real busy or visiting Uranus, they might talk to you, if they feel like it.

DOWN TO THE P.O.

Wouldn't you know that it was Mrs. Reverend Briscoe who would tell Wimsey Jump that his wife Hagar and Professor Shepherd were doing something un-Christian down to the P.O. when the window is closed at lunchtime? Professor Shepherd, as we all know, was teaching Good Literature when he lost his tenure at the college and had to start living on his boat down to the harbor, where things have been going downhill ever since.

We used to have the Post Office in the front room at old Miss Inez Bugg's house on Black Dog Road, but after she retired and moved to Arbutus to live with her daughter, the government built us the present P.O., which is an ugly red brick building with a flag out in front. The front room at Miss Inez's was a lot more interesting because when you went in to get your mail, you could smell what she and Mr. Frank had for dinner last night, and see whether she had watered her african violets and dusted the light up picture of Our Lady over the TV. Since the Buggs were Seventh Day Adventists, it was hard to figure out why the Virgin Mary was there, but it sure did give everyone something to talk about around here, like they didn't have enough already.

Hagar Jump is our postmaster now, and after she gets the mail up about eight-thirty, she posts a daily update on *The Young and The Restless* for those who have to work and miss the stories on TV, which many around here feel is a genuine community service, right up there with the fire department and the life support, especially

Chief Briscoe who got hooked on it while recovering from his piles operation.

Hagar likes having the new P.O. building, even though the old folks say it's just not the same. It's just that Wimsey would hate having the P.O. in his living room. Wimsey teaches algebra over to the high school and is home all summer puttering around with his garden. He likes to take a nap on the sofa in his underwear on hot afternoons, and you can't have ladies like Nettie Leery and Carlotta Hackett watching you snore in your tiger print boxers smelling like 10-05-10 and tomato vines when they're mailing out the VFD Newsletter. I would imagine, too, that the P.O. people have rules about that kind of thing. Nonetheless, Wimsey got mildly curious about what was going on, and left off planting his Silver Queen one afternoon to see what Hagar had got up to now. She fancies herself artistic, and sometimes Wimsey has to calm her down, you see.

As it happens, before he goes to his DNR clam checking job down to the harbor, Professor Shepherd drops by the P.O. to pick up his mail and ends up watching the stories with Hagar. Professor Shepherd is a man who is easily distracted, especially from checking the temperature of manose clams. I suspect, although we can't prove it, that they also read everyone's magazines before she puts them up. Why else is my *People* always a day late?

Anyway, when Wimsey went in the P.O. lobby at lunchtime, he could hear the two of them back there trying to figure out if Vicki and Cole will ever get back together or if Victor is really going to dig up Eve's body or not. Hagar told Professor Shepherd he ought to work for the stories because he's really good at predicting where the plots will go. He was the one who figured out Vicki was getting ready to turn into Nicki again on *One Life to Live* long before anyone else around here figured that Dorian didn't murder Victor.

From time to time, Professor Shepherd has tried to get Hagar interested in Good Literature, but he isn't having much luck with it. He tried to start her off with Eudora Welty and Flannery O'Connor, but it didn't take. "I didn't understand that *Why I Live at the P.O.*

story at all," she complained. "They would *never* let you live at the Post Office, and that Stella Rondo just ought to have been shaken, that's all. Now, *A Lady of Fashion* by Rebecca Baldwin, that was a good story. I like those Regency Romances. There's enough ugliness in real life, without having to write about it. When you work at the P.O. you just see all kinds of heartbreak and drama," she added darkly.

It makes you wonder whether she's been reading your bills through the envelopes, or sneaking a peak at those letters from your ex's lawyer over to Chestertown. We know she reads all the postcards that come in.

Good Literature hasn't been all that good to Professor Shepherd either. Maybe he ought to write one of those Regency Romances Hagar likes so much, because things have been really dull on the stories lately. So that on the day Wimsey came checking up, the two of them were sitting back there and waxing philosophical during the commercials.

"The ancient Greeks and Romans really blew it when they didn't create a God of Disappointment," Professor Shepherd told Hagar. "There ought to be at least a Patron Saint of Failed Hopes, somebody you could pray to before you get your mail in the morning. And the *sanctum locus* ought to be in the P.O. People get their mail every day with an optimism that is almost never fulfilled."

"Oh, my, yes, it's true," Hagar said wisely. "They come in here with such high hopes. Maybe today there will be a love note from your long lost sweetheart, or a letter from a lawyer in Texas announcing that you've inherited a cattle ranch and fifty oil wells from your third cousin once removed. Instead you get a past due notice from Sears on your washing machine and a postcard from Junior and Doreen Redmond who are having a great time in Hawaii without you. And you go home disappointed. It's enough to break your heart, you know."

"Now there's a situation that demands Divine Intervention. Maybe a human sacrifice," Professor Shepherd said. "We all need to propitiate the God of Disappointment, the Diety of Failed Expectations, keep it away from our mail. Mail, Hagar, is the last bastion of hope in this cruel world," he says.

Well, Wimsey understood then. He just got his power bill and the L.L. Bean catalogue out of the box and went on home to plant his Silver Queen corn. He knows now he doesn't have anything to worry about with those two, except that at the rate they're going, they just might write a Regency Romance about the God of Disappointment and sell the story to *The Young and The Restless*.

Wimsey's taught enough dumb-as-a-chunk high school kids math to know that there's a crying need for a God of Disappointment, no matter what Mrs. Reverend Briscoe says. But that Chris fellow over to the DNR says if Professor Shepherd doesn't get out there and check those clams, he's going to give the job to someone who won't disappoint him.

WE ALMOST DECLARED WAR
ON DELAWARE

*W*ell, here it is summer again and you know what that means. It's time for the annual Mosquito Festival here in Oysterback. If I, Desiree Grinch, proprietor of the Blue Crab Tavern, have to live through another Mosquito Festival like last year's, I think I will board up the bar and go to Capt. and Mrs. Lennie Skinner's rental cottage in Ocean City that weekend.

Now I realize that the Mosquito Festival brings in a lot of money for the VFD and the Community Center, and that we are a poor town and have to get what we can, where we can, but I also hope the current governor, whomever that is by the time you read this, will not almost declare war on Delaware like the one we had last year did.

I personally have nothing against our cousins in Slower Delaware, across the state line, and in fact, shop at Screaming Wally's Deep Discount Club every chance I get because there's no sales tax and the people watching around Dover AFB is the best I've seen since Tod Browning's film *Freaks*. Which is why some of us were pretty upset last year when our last year's governor and their last year's governor got into that fight at our very own Mosquito Festival and our governor had to be dissuaded from declaring war on Delaware.

I mean, don't you think the mosquito can be the bird of both states? There certainly are plenty of *Culicidae* to go around without two middle-aged men in seersucker suits and striped ties standing on a bandstand swatting at each other over the question of who can claim them as a state symbol. I guess it's a good thing the governor

of Virginia wasn't there, or this whole peninsula would have been nuked like one of those microwave hot dogs over to Ray Bob's Gas 'n' Go.

Lamont L'Eureux, the Ragin' Cajun, may not be back, either. Last year, he hauled straight through the interstates from Cou de Rouge, rolling 80 all the way in his Proud Coon Ass Contractors Inc. truck, bringing us coolers of red and white boudin, crayfish, shrimp, Wonderbread, and his mama's dirty rice, as well as his champion mosquito, Miss Budweiser XXVII, out of Miss Budweiser XXVI by Bayou Bob. Lamont's got a stud ditch on his farm in Jefferson Parish, and since Miss Genvieve started computerizing those bloodlines in her spare time down at the Piggly Wiggly, Lamont's been the acknowledged breeder of champions. He doesn't even race any more; he just goes around to all the festivals to do the yearling sales and improve his breeding stock. He didn't even look twice at the battling governors. Where he comes from, politicians shoot each other over little points like that. Which may be why all hell broke loose when he was holding Miss Budweiser XXVII in his hand, showing her to Huddie and Junie, and something happened. It seems that state delegate Orville Orvall thought he was a new voter and rushed over to give him a hearty handclasp. Oh, well.

I guess Orville won't do that twice; the skin graft doctors at Hopkins won't let him, for one thing.

Speaking of medical attention, it was a good thing Dr. Wheedleton was there when Ranger Jay from Scales and Tales was showing the program's rehabilitated raptors to the Boone Brothers, who got a little put out, them being the owners of the Boone Bros We Fix & Road Kill Cooked Here Cafe over to Tubman's Corners. They sort of feel Scales and Tales is competing with them, I guess. And Gabe and Mike were in bad moods anyway because their hand-dipped Skeeter Chocolate Bites didn't go over too well.

Well, our Celebrity Guest Finish Line for the big Skeeter Derby was Ricki Lake, so that was all right. I heard she complained about all the mosquito bites, but she's big into animal rights, so I don't understand her problem. I don't know who we're getting for

Celebrity Guest this year. We'd like to get Kato Kaelin, but Omar Hinton's afraid he might not leave when it's over. I suggested my current personal favorite Courtney Love, the Widow Cobain, but her fifteen minutes might be up by this weekend.

I just hope this year the Patamoke Community Theatre in the Oblong doesn't decide to do that flea circus musical about that singing fly. I mean, how many people want to see an opera called *Mosca*?

DEAD AND BREAKFAST

Miss Sister Gibbs thinks you have to move with the times to stay young, but not too fast. This summer she retired after forty years of teaching to become the resident manager of the Ye Olde Colonial Watershed Bed and Breakfast.

I, Desiree Grinch, proprietor of the Blue Crab Tavern, say it's like Mrs. Danvers retiring from Manderly to run Tara. She'll just have a whole new set of people to scare the living daylights out of. I mean, Miss Sister is one tough lady. They say she smiled once, back in the '30s, but I'm not too sure about that.

Junie Redmond and Huddie Swann, who have to make a joke out of everything, go around calling it the Ye Olde Colonial Bloodshed because it used to be the old Gersen place where all those tourists were murdered happened back in the '60s. But even they don't call it the Ye Olde Colonial Bloodshed in front of Miss Sister; she used to teach eighth grade, and that tour of duty left her with a whim of iron and a glare that can turn you to stone. Miss Sister says jump, you say how high, if you know what I mean and I think you do.

Anyway, that old house just sat out there on Mad Calf Lane rotting away until the West Hundred Daughters of Historical Lineage got a hold of it and turned it into the Patamoke Designer House a couple of years ago. They had the Two Guys from Annapolis Interior Design Firm come in and supervise the decorators. Charles and Reynaldo did the living room themselves, and it won some kind of prize for the best use of green and pink in the same room.

"We're just couple of Martha Stewart queens," Reynaldo said, but I think he's just being modest; the place really did look good after they finished up with it, and was featured in many of the local Sunday supplements. Those decorators did a real good job of covering up the bloodstains.

In fact, the old Gersen place looked so good that some bridge and tunnel people from Potomac bought the place from the Hysterical, I mean, Historical Daughters (another Junie and Huddie-ism) and opened the Olde Colonial Watershed Bed and Breakfast. I don't know if it was they weren't ready for the service industry's many petty humiliations, or the ghostly screams of Old Man Gersen's victims echoing through the Retro Jacobite wallpapered halls, but those bridge and tunnel people weren't here too long before they moved to St. Michaels, where you can buy the past in a microwavable package. With an historically accurate hot tub that Alexander Hamilton used himself.

Well, that place sat on the market for a while, until the Two Guys from Annapolis heard about it, and Charles and Reynaldo came back and bought it from those Potomac people for a song. They told everyone that it was the old Gersen place, and that a lot of people had been murdered there in one of the most sensational homicides in Maryland history. "We may be a couple of Martha Stewart queens, but we know how to market to the '90s," Charles told me.

Miss Sister was available, so they placed her in charge. "She just goes with the ambiance," Reynaldo explained sweetly.

"Early mortuary?" I asked.

Reynaldo just laughed. "Late X-Files," he replied.

I'll be the first to admit that it worked. That place is packed with morbid sensation seekers every weekend. But I haven't heard anyone complaining about ghostly screams disturbing their peace in their French Tudor bedrooms.

They'd be afraid to, I guess. If Miss Sister could wrangle eighth-graders all those years and strike the fear of God into humans at the most uncivilized phase of their development, some whiney old ghosts aren't about to scare her. I'll bet they came out, all ready to scream and moan, took one look at her and faded quietly away, apologizing as they went. All Miss Sister had to to do was give them one of those basilisk schoolteacher looks of hers and they sank right back into the carefully stripped and stippled woodwork.

"Isn't she just too wonderful?" Reynaldo sighed.

"The guests just love her! So...so dire!" Charles nodded.

Easy for them to say. They never had her for eighth grade.

☉YSTERBACK 🦀 BUGEYE

| Helga Wallop, Editor | PO Box 3, Oysterback MD 21000 | 25 cents |

🦀 *Published every now and then or whenever there's news...* 🦀

BETTER READ THAN DEAD

Weddings, Obituaries, and Other Near-Death Experiences From Oysterback

Following an unfortunate incident, Gabe and Mike Boone have announced that they will not be serving Groundhog Casserole next February 2nd at the We Fix & Road Kill Cooked Here Cafe and Garage. Dr. Sam Wheedleton suggests anyone still suffering adverse effects contact his office immediately.

Johnny Ray Insley, having recovered from his near-death experience after totaling the police cruiser while doing traffic duty for Tuesday Nite Bingo at St. Morphemes' over to Patamoke, will be speaking about his adventures in the afterlife at the Community Center next Thursday. Johnny Ray reports that Ariana Huffington appeared to him at the end of a long tunnel of light and told him to get hair plugs.

Chickadee Dachstedder and Norris Peavine were married in a double-ring ceremony Saturday at Oysterback Hardshell Methodist Church. The bride and groom wore matching fringed white leather outfits designed by the bride's mother, Mrs. Jodi Dachstedder of Jodi's Fashion Whirl in Wallopsville. The couple are both in the entertainment business; the new Mrs. Peavine, who is 1995 Delmarva Soybean Queen, is also a sales rep for radio station WDEV and Mr. Peavine owns Mello-Groov D.J. Party Services of Tubman's Corners, Inc. After a honeymoon trip to Harper's Ferry, the couple will reside in the mother-in-law apartment behind the groom's father's chicken houses on Mad Calf Lane.

Ricketts and Georgelane Schtubb are suing Claymore and Velraye Gibbs because their new deck blocks the morning sun in the east corner of the Schtubb's bedroom and are also pressing charges against anyone who disagrees with their politics. The Schtubbs moved here from Oxford.

In related news, Judge Findlay Fish says the court docket is getting right backed up and he hasn't ruled anyone in contempt for at least a week now.

Obald R. "Pink" Blatterwack, long-time resident of Wallopsville, passed away unexpectedly at the age of 96 at the Loblolly Senile Dementia Residential Treatment Facility, formerly

(See Dead p. 2)

(Dead from p. 1)

the Loblolly Home before Devanau Medical Center, formerly County General Hospital, took it over and raised the insurance rates. Formerly proprietor of Pink's Bait Boutique, he was an avid spades player and bird watcher and was best known for his lifelist of Elliott's Island black rails. Born in Mannheim, Germany, he was universally known throughout the West Hundred as the *"foreigner* foreigner." Arrangements by Dreedle Funeral Home.

Speaking of celebrity dreams, and we were, Whack Wallace is marketing her new Dream Steam Facial Masque, receipt given to her in a dream by Newt Gingrich. He told her to make it from chamomile and eucalyptus leaves. It's on sale down to the Curl Up 'n' Dye Salon de Beaute.

Sheriff Wesley Briscoe has apprehended the Wallopsville Laundry Lifter, who turned out to be Delegate Orville Orvall, home from Annapolis to explain his vote on the car insurance bill to angry voters. Anyone missing laundry off their clotheslines should come down to the Community Center Tuesday night and pick out what's theirs, especially those leopardskin his and hers bikini underwears.

The Oysterback Volunteer Fire Department's annual trip to the fireman's convention in Ocean City was pronounced a smashing success by newly elected President for Life Junior Redmond. The entire fire company were guests of Captain and Mrs. Lennie Skinner at their rental cottage on 72nd Street. Special guests included the Ocean City Police where First Lieutenant for Life Poot Wallop fortunately has a cousin. Chief for Life Hudson Swann won the wet t-shirt contest.

The Battle of the Bulge will be rehashed again this year when Omar and Thelma Hinton go with Omar's old war buddy Herb Hightower and wife Grace to a 101st Airborne Division reunion in New Orleans. As usual, Thelma reports, she and Grace will be fighting their own Battle of the Bulge trying to keep their soldier boys on their high-fiber, low-fat diets amidst all that Cajun and Creole cooking.

Hooley Legume, Oysterback's most famous major league outfielder, who has nothing better to do these days, will be minding Omar's store, so remember to count your change. Hooley says if the strike keeps up, he might have to sell one of his three houses and the Land Rover.

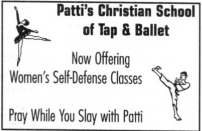

BETTER THE DEVIL YOU KNOW

It was hot for June, one of those blank, humid days that come during a long dry spell. The dust lay on the road and across the fields, coating the limp and thirsty soybeans with clay grit. It was so hot that the usual collection of retired watermen and farmers had moved themselves outside of Omar Hinton's store and on to the old wooden benches under the shade of the overhang, hoping to catch the memory of a breeze from the river.

Omar himself had come out and taken a seat, next to Hardee Swann. After the lunch rush, business was dead, and he was catching a cat nap under the latest *Bugeye*, featuring a picture of Miss Carlotta Hackett giving an Historical Daughters Plaque to Venus Tutweiler. It rose and fell on his gentle snores.

Faraday Hicks rode up on his John Deere mower. He was gloating about his own cleverness in eluding his daughter as he extracted a chew from his tobacco pouch. Bosley Grinch and Wilbur Rivers were just sitting, nursing their R.C. Colas, squinting out across the fields into the hard, colorless sunlight. Ferrus T. Buckett occupied himself carving the head of a merganser from a chunk of scrap pine.

No one was talking; for one thing it was too hot, and for another, there was nothing to say. Weather, crabs, crops, gossip, and the government had already been dispatched. The ability of old men to sit in companionable silence for long periods of time has been honed to a fine art in Oysterback. It gives the younger people something to look forward to, and the old men are aware they have to set an example for the coming generation.

When a sullen little dust devil came twisting up the road, all beige dust and dry leaves, no one stirred. When it stopped before the overhang, forming itself into the shape of a cloven-hoofed, scarlet-skinned demon, replete with horns, tail, and flashy yellow eyes, the old men barely raised an eyebrow, although the faint stench of fire, brimstone, and perfume ads from the glossier magazines hung in the still air. The apparition turned fiery amber eyes on the assemblage, drawing itself up to a pretty good height and breadth.

"KNOW YE THAT I AM SATAN!" he exclaimed self-importantly.

Faraday Hicks spit a long stream of tobacco juice. Hardee Swann half opened one eye. Ferrus never even looked up from his carving. The *Bugeye* on top of Omar's face crackled a little as he let out a particularly loud snort. Wilbur Rivers scratched himself in an impolite place and Bosley Grinch tore open his Little Debbie Snack package with his few remaining real teeth.

"I AM SATAN!" that gentleman repeated, speaking a little louder now just in case they hadn't gotten it the first time. You never know with old men; they might not hear too well.

"Used to be a family around here named Saddin, but they moved," Hardee Swann yawned.

"Bought a farm over to Shaft Ox Corner," Omar volunteered from beneath the *Bugeye*. "One of the girls married a Glack."

"I AM LUCIFER!" the devil roared, but he was starting to sound just a shade uncertain about it.

"Nah, *Lucy* Santana married one of the Pusey boys from over to Tubman's Corners. It was *Phyllis* who married Dembo Glack."

"Dembo was the one who fell out of the Tilt-A-Whirl at the Harrington Fair that time. His cousin Widge was the Glack that Phyllis married. They had Glack's Good Oil and Propane over to...."

"I AM THE LORD OF HELL!" Satan exclaimed, and tried to produce some special effects to prove it, but it was already so hot that no one noticed the fire and sparks.

"That young fella say he was related to those Lords over to Marydel?" Bosley asked Faraday Hicks, inclining his head toward the devil, who was sullenly kicking a hoof at the old bottle caps and oystershells into the road like a thwarted, show-off kid.

"No," Faraday slowly replied after some thought, "that's not their name, it's Loud, or Lloyd, or something like that. But she was a granddaughter of Old Man Lumpkind, the one that had alla them German POW's picking fruit for him during the war...."

"Maybe it was the Lumpkinds I was thinking of," Hardee admitted grudgingly. He shifted his upper plate as he squinted at the stranger. "You looking for the Lumpkind place, son?"

"I AM SATAN!" The devil stamped his hoof in frustration, shell and bottle caps scattering. "What's *wrong* with you people? Don't you watch TV? I'm the Great Satan. The Ultimate Evil. The Prince of Darkness."

"I had a dog named Prince once," Bosley Grinch sighed around a mouthful of Snack Cake. "That dog wouldn't hunt, neipert way."

Omar's newspaper was shaking gently; he was really trying to stifle himself under there.

By that time, Hagar Jump had come to the door of the P.O. and was staring across the road, looking as if she were just about to head over and investigate. Hagar was notoriously interested in other people's business.

"Aw, come on, guys," Satan pleaded. "Help me out here."

Ferrus sighted down the bill of his merganser head. "You go on down the road about four miles, and turn west. Can't miss it," he said. "There's a big sign out on the road."

"Thank you," the devil said stiffly. In less time than it takes to tell, he was gone, perfume ads and all, in a cloud of dust.

"What was that all about?" Hagar called as she came across the road, fanning herself with a Buy 'N' Bag Supermarket flyer. She stared down the road at the disappearing cloud of dust, then back at the men on the benches, who were looking entirely too innocent to suit her.

"Oh, just some lost tourist looking for Route 50," Omar replied. Carefully, he rolled up the *Bugeye* and used it to swat a mosquito that had landed on his arm.

"If I owned Route 50 and hell," Hardee Swann said solemnly, "I'd rent out Route 50 and live in hell."

"Amen to that," Faraday spit.

FATHERHOOD

*T*he first chance he got, Hudson Swann started to teach his daughters how to drive. When they were very little, he would drive up and down the road at a snail pace, holding them in his lap, letting them pretend to steer his Ford pickup.

In the long summer evenings after dinner, while Jeanne has her quiet time with bubble bath and *Country Living*, Hudson, Amber, and Ashley pile into the truck and drive down to Omar Hinton's store for ice cream cones. Ashley steers and Amber works the pedals on the way down; it's the opposite on the way back. Being twins and having that bond, it seems to work out well between them. Hudson coaches from the passenger seat. He's pretty proud of their progress. By the time they're big enough to reach the pedals by themselves, he thinks they'll do all right. Hudson believes everyone should know three things: how to swim, how to drive a car, and how to read. The rest, he says, will fall into place.

Over to Omar Hinton's store, all the watermen and farmers are lounging around under the big ceiling fan, trying to stay cool. Warner, Omar's old black lab, is stretched out under the stove, where the cold metal feels good on hot nights. When he hears Ashley and Amber coming, he gets up and finds his old tennis ball. With Warner, hope springs eternal. Black labs put up with a lot on the Eastern Shore.

Hudson buys the twins the exact same thing every night: one scoop of vanilla, one scoop of chocolate on a wafer cone, done twice.

He gets himself a single scoop of Butter Brickle and settles down on the bench while the twins and Warner toss the old tennis ball up and down the cereal aisle. It's about all the excitement Warner can handle these days, Omar says. The truth is, it's about all the excitement Omar can stand.

Ashley and Amber have decided when they grow up, they are leaving Oysterback to launch careers as a fairy princess and a mermaid, respectively. Amber also wants to be an MTV star in her spare time. Ashley is starting to lean toward becoming an artist like her big sister Duc Tran; she likes Duc's pierced nose. Eating ice cream cones and half listening to watermen over to Omar Hinton's store complain about the DNR and Washington is a temporary condition for them. They know there's a world out there waiting for them.

They also know enough to say "thank you" when Omar gives them each a biscuit for Warner. Warner can balance a dog biscuit on the end of his nose until you tell him "go"; then he flips it in the air and catches it in his teeth. Warner thinks it's a pretty stupid trick, but he likes the biscuits.

When the cones are finished, the twins go over to their father and crawl all over him until he realizes they're there and it's time to go. Then they all get into the truck again and start for home. This time Amber steers and Ashley works the pedals, and Hudson looks out the window at the soy bean fields and pine woods going by in the fading summer twilight

When he sees a herd of deer, six or seven does and their fawns grazing at the edge of the field by the woods in the twilight, he makes the girls stop the car and they all stare at the deer. The deer stare back, like it's a contest, a Mexican standoff, to see who can look the longest. After a few minutes, a big sixteen-point buck comes along and urges the herd back into the darkening thicket. There are a few graceful deer movements and then it's as if they were never there; just a few quivering branches and then, nothing. That's what deer are like, Hudson says, the last magical animals.

At that moment, he has a new thought; that he will remember this moment forever—his daughters as children, the bright orange trumpet vine that crawls along the fence, the distant sound of a redwing blackbird, those deer at twilight on this road. He folds this away in his memory like an heirloom, something to be brought out for special occasions. Not for the first time, he is awed by this circumstance of being a father, by the idea that children are hostages to fortune. That we all must do the best we can with what we have, whether we are deer or daddies. Cliches, he decides, have the terrible weight of truth.

Next, he decides, it will be time to show them how to run the boat. Celestial navigation is a good thing to know.

WIMSEY JUMP HAS AN ADVENTURE

In June, as every kid knows, teachers get put in a closet with the textbooks, where they go into suspended animation until next September. Some of us who have a little more age on us and actually know people who teach, recognize the truth. Down here on the Shore, if teachers aren't in school themselves over the summer, they can become temporary cops in Ocean City, or they can work at Wal-Mart. Or, if they're Wimsey Jump, who teaches algebra, they can sign on with Huddie and Junie's grass cutting service, where they can ride around on great big rider mowers all day, cutting the enormous, environmentally comatose lawns of rich weekend people.

When you can't make enough working the water to pay your boat, opening a grass cutting business is the waterman's next choice. Maybe there's something about riding around in your pickup dragging a trailerload of John Deere's and Cub Cadettes that fulfills some primal genetic urge, or maybe it's the basic testosterone siren call of machines. Those who know say you just can't have more manly a time than a day spent straddling the GrassMaster 5 HP, 9 gear Lawn Brute 2000. It's not quite a babe magnet, but having that amount of machine under you will command the respect of your peers, which is more the point with real men and some real women, too. Ask Wimsey.

One hot day in June, when the humidity made breathing the air the equivalent of sucking in a bowl of lime Jell-O, Junie, Huddie, and Wimsey were cutting grass on the estate of one of our ten-cent

millionaires. Weekend people. You know the type: they have a great big new waterfront house, come here two days a week, live down a long wooded lane, and couldn't find the local issues with two hands and a roadmap, but never hesitate to stomp into Omar Hinton's store to complain about the lack of bicycle lanes on Red Toad Road and brie cheese in his deli case. But they've got three acres of growing lawn, so Junie calls them cash cows. And some other stuff I can't print here.

Anyway, after a couple of hours on the Lawn Brute in shadeless ninety-six degree heat, the smell of gas and oil fumes and the pricking of a thousand freshly cut shards of grass on bare skin can get to a man. So when Wimsey made a pass around the pool (all ten-cent millionaires have swimming pools) he saw that Huddie and Junie were already stripped to their farmer tans and cannonballing off the diving board. "Come on in," Junie yelled. "They won't never know! They only come on weekends!"

Wimsey didn't have to be told twice. As quick as it takes to type this sentence, he was stripped and plunged into that cool blue water.

Man thought he'd died and gone to heaven, that pool felt so wet and so cool and so blissful.

Now, you know Junie and Huddie, and you know that they are fond of a joke. While Wimsey was doing the backstroke, they climbed out of that pool, dressed, gathered up Wimsey's clothes, loaded up the mowers, and roared down the driveway. Laughing all the way.

When Wimsey poked his head up, he saw the trailer end of Junie's truck heading south, missed his clothes, and decided that they were playing a good joke on him. So, he lay back in the water and floated for a while, waiting for them to come back. What the hell, Wimsey figured, he would have done the same to either of them, and he was getting paid by the hour.

It was only when Wimsey heard a car door slam and looked over the edge of the pool toward the house, and saw the ten-cent millionaire family unloading their Mercedes that he figured it out: Junie and Huddie must have passed the owner's family on their way in and they weren't coming back!

Poor Wimsey! He allowed his head to sink below the side of the pool and hoped no one wanted to swim, although he had a bad moment when their golden, one of the stupidest dogs in the world, came over to lick the top of his salty, sunburned head.

By and by, as the shadows began to lengthen, Wimsey began to get a little uneasy. His fingers and toes were turning into prunes, and it was getting right boring, having to duck his head under water every time someone walked past the window by the pool. When Wimsey heard the sound of the family eating—the smell of food, those knives and forks clanging against china plates—he decided it was a good time to be gone. So he hoisted his naked algebra teacher's body out of the pool and headed for the shrubbery, skulking his way from boxwood to boxwood, trying to make a break for the woods and the road to Oysterback beyond. Surely Junie and Huddie were parked at the foot lane, waiting for him!

Consider the feelings of the man as he skulked, barefoot and buck naked, through the greenbriar and the loblolly pines. Wimsey Jump, a man with a master's degree, a teacher, exposing his forty-three-year-old body to the curious stare of fox squirrels and deers. Maybe Huddie and Junie wouldn't think much of such a plight, but for a man like Wimsey, who spends nine months of the year indoors, the whole thing was disturbing. The indignity of it was almost too much for him, but the green flies and the mosquitoes were worse, so he plunged on through the trees, and headed toward the road.

When he peered out of the birch at the ditchbank, looking up the road then down, his heart sank. There was no sign of Junie's truck anywhere! Then he saw it. He knew they wouldn't abandon him entirely. The GrassMaster sat waiting for him, the key in the ignition.

Unfortunately, Junie and Huddie, in their haste to escape, had neglected to leave his clothes, not even his shorts!

Luckily, Red Toad Road isn't a busy route to anywhere. Most God-fearing people who don't have fools for friends were home eating dinner anyway. The GrassMaster started up with a roar, and still in a state of nature, Wimsey headed toward home, already framing up how he would retaliate, formulating the prank he planned for Junie and Huddie. He was so engrossed in where he could find a Klingon costume and a fake FBI identification card, he never heard the little Toyota pull cautiously up beside him.

"Uh, is that you, Mr. Jump?" someone called, and Wimsey looked over to see one of his students, Josh Somebody or Another, looking him up and down with eyes as big as saucers.

Wimsey nodded. "Hello, Josh," he said with what he hoped was proper teacher authority. Since that was all he had to pull around his shredded dignity, he went with it.

"Uh, Mr. Jump, would you like to borrow my swim trunks?" Josh asked uncertainly. In the passenger seat, Wimsey caught a glimpse of a teenage girl, eyes also as wide as saucers. He had to shut down the GrassMaster to cross one hairy white, scratched up, mosquito-bitten leg over the other.

"Yes, please," Wimsey said shortly. Without a word, Josh reached into the back seat, then handed Wimsey a damp pair of

Hawaiian print jams. Wimsey accepted them with a muttered thanks.

Josh swallowed. "Uh, Mr. Jump," he said uncertainly. "Uh, you won't tell anyone you saw us on Red Toad Road, will you?"

Wimsey nodded. "Of course not," he agreed. The jams smelled faintly of mildew.

Josh grinned with relief. "Thanks Mr. Jump! You're one cool dude!" The girl waved.

Wimsey waited until the Toyota was well out of sight before he slipped on the shorts and headed home.

It wasn't until about two weeks later, after he'd gotten Huddie and Junie back good, that Wimsey wondered exactly what Josh and the girl were doing on Red Toad Road. Given the activities of high school students these days, he's decided he really doesn't want to know.

BLUE HOUR

Chelsea Redmond has set up a snowcone stand down by the harbor this summer, and it's been quite a hit with both the watermen and the tourists, especially when the temperature reaches for the hundreds and the humidity lies so thick on the ground that you could take a jackhammer to it and not make a dent in the atmosphere. For seventy-five cents, you can get a wax paper cup full of chipped ice and some exotic, sugary flavoring like Mango Peach or Limon Breeze or Blue Hawaii, then sit in the shade of a few sullen pin oaks at one of the picnic tables watching life pass you by, spooning in icy sugar and chemicals you'd probably rather not know the names of, even if you could pronounce them. The interesting thing is, those syrups are quite refreshing on these humid evenings; even the little yellow wasps think so as they angrily buzz around you, driven nuts by the smell of the sweetness.

If you know Ferrus T. Buckett real well, and he's in a good mood, he'll add a tablespoon of Pride of Baltimore Vodka to your snowcone, from the pint bottle he keeps in the cuddy of his workboat for emergencies like hot summer evenings when the shadows grow long and purple. If you don't, you're out of luck, of course. Ferrus is baiting up lines, not running a bar.

Not that there are all that many crabs to be caught this summer, and only another six weeks of hot weather, and that's what Huddie Swann and Junie Redmond and Earl Don Grinch and Paisley Redmond and Professor Shepherd are all talking about as they lean into the sides of Junie's '86 Chevy Sierra pickup, staring into the junky bottom of the flatbed like the true meaning of life is to be found in some old nylon rope, a half dozen bushel basket lids, and a bag of aluminum cans Junie keeps forgetting to drop off at the recycling station on his way into town. Actually, they aren't talking, they're communicating in a series of sophisticated grunts and trying to hide their beer cans from the interested gaze of Lt. Georgia Pickett of the Natural Resources Police, who is off duty and frankly couldn't care less. She just wants to sit with her kids and her boyfriend at a picnic table and eat her macaroni salad and have her day off in peace.

If leaning into the flatbed of a pick up for hours on end, resting your elbows on the sides of the truck, and communicating in sophisticated grunts were an Olympic event, Eastern Shore men would bring home the gold everytime. Of course, there's a whole set of etiquette to it, with rules as complex and subtle as a *levée du roi* at

Versailles, but Georgia doesn't feel like thinking about that right now and neither do I; it's just too hot and humid.

But there is a faint breeze off the river that makes being down at the harbor almost bearable now that the sun's setting, and it seems like lots of folks have the same idea, because they're here too, lounging around on the grass or half-heartedly picking at things to do on their boats because it's too hot to fish and there's not enough air to sail. Just about right, though, to get an apple cinnamon snow cone and gossip with your neighbor in the next slip about the weekend people on the other side of you who have had the strangest parade of company coming through all summer, the oddest human beings you could imagine. The one girl, well, she wasn't really a girl, she must have been about thirty-five, who walked down the main street to the water wearing nothing but a red bathing suit, what did she think this was, Ocean City? You can bet that caused some talk around here. And the man with the green hair who ran breathlessly into Omar Hinton's store asking Omar (of all people!) for *baguettes* and *fromage bleu*, as if this were an outpost of Sutton Place Gourmet.

Darkly, someone says they ought to put a big fence around the District, Prince George's, and Montgomery Counties and keep all those Washingtonians in there and away from normal people, because those yupwheats—that's the word we all use now, yupwheats—are really obnoxious, especially that guy from the *Post* who wrote that piece about us, whining about how you couldn't buy arugula around here. But it's too hot to even fuss about the yupwheats and their weird diets and boorish manners.

So, try a Mortal-Coil-Chocolate-Banana-flavored snowcone and let the ice melt on the back of your tongue, feeling the wet chill running down your throat. Treat yourself to some marshmallow on top, a new innovation this year, something Chelsea picked up while in Stone Harbor visiting her Mum-Mum and Pop-Pop Crawford.

Delmar P. and Earlene come riding up on the Harley, that big old '62 Electraglide Delmar's been working back into order all summer. While Earlene buys a couple of Cosi Fan Tutti Frutti snowcones and talks with Georgia about Sunshine Sisters, Delmar P. unloads his accordion off the back of the hog and ambles out to the end of the jetty, where the setting sun silhouettes his big bulky frame. From back here, he looks like one of Claude Crouch's visionary chainsaw sculptures: Neanderthal Man with Squeeze Box.

Just when you want to say that out loud and maybe get a cheap laugh, Delmar lets loose with some of his blues riffs, and the quarter notes just carry themselves back on the breeze, filling up the whole harbor with that slide-back-and-get-down juke joint accordion studying "Lonesome Sundown Blues." Delmar can make that old box sound just like Bessie Smith, wailing about lost love and loneliness until it's a magic moment that makes everyone stop and listen, even the little kids. Maybe even the fish in the river like to listen when Delmar P. plays the blues on the blue hour of a summer twilight. Maybe the deer at the edge of the soybean field across the river stop eating, big ears twitching as they fill up with the sound of Delmar P. playing the "Lonesome Sundown Blues." You could even imagine the ghosts awakening for the night's haunt, snapping their dry, brittle fingerbones to the beat of Delmar's blues accordion at sunset, ordering a Vanilla Wafer snowcone with marshmallow topping because this is definitely worth coming back from the dead for; this is what the essence of life is all about, moments like this.

The sun slowly sets behind the marsh. Then, with the distant roar of a billion angry wings, the huge black cloud of mosquitoes rises up off the flats, looking for blood. First, people start slapping their bare, bitten skin. Then one by one, they begin to gather up their things to go home. They slip away into the gray darkness where they'll be safe behind the screens, where the air conditioners will shut out the wet world.

After a while, only Delmar P. is left, playing the accordion blues until it's so dark he can't see the keys. But long after even he's gone home, the music lingers on the summer air, so humid and thick it can carry a tune home in a bucket, and stop en route to buy a Creamsicle Orange snowcone.

Autumn

WELCOME TO
OYSTERBACK

POP: 687

SUPREMELY TRASHY

*D*id you know that those Supreme Court Justices used to live at Shallow Shores Doublewide Park? It's true! They rented Dontay Hicks' house after he and Doris retired to Homosassa Springs.

Mostly, they kept to themselves, but you couldn't help but notice them. They weren't what you would call "good" neighbors. At first, we thought they might be one of those weird religious cults, what with those black robes and the way they called Rehnquist "Chief," but then we found out they were lawyers and that was even worse.

Right away, we knew there was going to be trouble because Ginsburg's Monster Mudder, Big Judge, had a bad muffler. She would wake up the whole neighborhood when she rolled in at two or three in the morning from the Mud Bogs over to Buck. Sheriff Briscoe had to speak to her about it, but only after enough people complained.

Thomas and O'Connor didn't exactly endear themselves around here either. The two of them were always hitting the yard sales, and they were the worst early birds you ever saw, always getting there around 4:30 a.m. Maybe Ginsburg woke 'em up! That time of day, people weren't even awake, let alone putting their stuff out, and those two would grab up all the good stuff, triple the prices, and put it in *their own* yard sale, which seemed to be held every single Saturday morning, which brought a lot of traffic through here, which we didn't appreciate.

We didn't think much of the way Souter collected trashed-out lead sled Chryslers in the back yard, or the dead washing machine that he left on the front porch to rust away. They must have found a new washing machine someplace, because on Sunday you'd see all those black robes hung out to dry on the line, which offended a lot of the older folks around here who don't believe in doing chores on a Sunday. Souter always had all these car parts spread out everywhere, but he never seemed to have a car that ran; you'd always see him hitchiking.

Scalia must have been lucky in his hunting. He had a big old board tied to the front grille of his truck, and from time to time, you'd see him dressing out a deer in the front, not the *back* yard, which is just common sorry. One time, he slaughtered a live hog out there; the smell was intense, and lingered for days. Some of the little ones had nightmares after that, let me tell you. And his dogs kept getting out and turning over trashcans all around the neighborhood, too!

And the noise? I'm here to tell you those Justices could make some loudness. First Monday in October, they always had this big party, and all these low-life lawyer types would be hanging around. Well, I don't need to tell you, we don't want that sort hanging around the neighborhood. Those lawyers are just plain bad news, and I don't care what anyone says, you can educate 'em 'til you're blue in the face, but the attorney always comes out in them. And dissent? I can't count the times Sheriff Briscoe had to come over there and break up the fights! He threatened 'em with the Domestic Intervention Program and they quieted down some after that, but every once in a while, they'd go off on each other, using the worst language you ever heard, words like "jurisprudence," and "precedent," and a lot of stuff in some foreign language that sounded like Latin, only worse.

It wasn't unusual to see Kennedy and all of them out there just sort of hanging around the porch until all hours, drinking out of cooler cups and saying the worst things, like "habeous corpus" or "ipso jure" right in front of the kids! And he'd have five or six carloads of those lawyers in the driveway with all their radios blasting out gansta rap and George Strait, and all those paralegals hanging around looking real suspicious. We've heard stories about people like that, and we don't want 'em around here.

Also, a lot of us wondered where they were putting nine adult people in those three tiny little bedrooms. Doreen Redmond got as far as the living room once when she was collecting for United Fund, and she said it looked like Breyer and Stevens slept on couches in the living room, and they had hung old sheets to the windows! She also said it was amazing how people could decorate with plastic flowers and cable spool coffee tables, and that it smelled like they cooked a lot of scrapple and muskrat in there. O'Connor said they had about five cats, so you can just imagine. But to judge by the wrappers and Styrofoam boxes you saw blowing around the yard, they mostly lived on Burger Clown and Snickers bars and Mountain Dew.

Mostly what we saw from the outside was all the yard orna-
ments, the plastic gnomes and pink flamingoes and whirligigs that
Stevens was always putting up, although you never saw him pick
up a piece of paper or a beer can. Thomas got one of those tire
planters, and Souter planted some scraggly geraniums in it and,
once in a while, you'd see Rehnquist out there mowing the lawn in
his Pink Floyd t-shirt, but not often enough to suit the other folks
at Shallow Shores, who are quite houseproud.

Toward June, there was this bunch of noise in the middle of the
night, and all their trucks and cars were coming and going until
dawn. In the morning, when it was strangely quiet, we looked over
there. We thought maybe they'd killed each other, but the place was
deserted. They'd done a midnight move!

Dontay had to come up then; said they still owed him three
months back rent, and they'd taken all the copper pipes, the light
fixtures, and everything else that wasn't nailed down. They left him
that old washing machine, a '71 New Yorker without a tranny, and a
pile of bald truck tires and about six or seven bags of trash to haul
away. A lot of us thought it served Dontay right for staying down
there in Florida and not paying attention, so he didn't get a whole lot
of sympathy from us.

A while back, we heard they were living in one of those welfare
hotels in New York Avenue in Washington, but we're not sure. One
thing we know, they'll never come back here; Sheriff's got a warrant
on them. Dontay says no good deed goes unpunished, and that he'll
be more careful who he rents to the next time, but we'll just have to
wait and see.

☆OYSTERBACK BUGEYE

| Helga Wallop, Editor | PO Box 3, Oysterback MD 21000 | 25 cents |

🦀 *Published every now and then or whenever there's news...* 🦀

All Politics is Local
LOFS Nest 10811 Names New President

Soon after Chris Parks started editing a newspaper down the Shore, he called us up here and mentioned that during the first town meeting he covered, the mayor had hit one of the aldermen with a chair. We at the *Bugeye* asked our fellow member of the fifth estate how he wrote that up? Parks said he didn't bother; it happens every week.

In a rare display of non-partisan politics, the Wallopsville town council voted 6-0 against passing a law that would make it a crime to stalk and harass the management of West Hundred Cable. This action followed the cable company's satellite glitch which caused all thirty-eight stations to run fifty-two hours of uninterrupted Trinity Broadcasting Network programming featuring Paul and Jan Crouch soliciting donations from the public to maintain their personal ministry's supply of lavender rinse and hairspray.

While speaking at the Scrapple and Muskrat Dewey Day Dinner over in Patamoke, Rick Kollinger reports that he ran into Orville Orvall, formerly our man in the state lege, and that Orville said he is planning to run again. For office this time, not from Sheriff Wesley Briscoe or the process servers. Rick says this means the West Hundred will have to look for a new village idiot.

God opened His car trunk of mercy and pulled out His spare tire of grace when the Reverend Foster Turbot persuaded the Devanau County Zoning Board to pass a one time only trash incineration exemption for the First Church of Elvis to hold a mortgage burning over on Black Dog Road (County Road 313).

The West Hundred Loyal Order of Fox Squirrels has elected Bunker Krankheit as 1998-99 president of Nest 10811. Krankheit, who succeeded the late Obald "Pink" Bladderwack as interim president, is known throughout the region as the owner-captain of the popular head boat Miss Foxy Lady VI and the owner of the Krankheit Beer and Liquor Distributorship.

James A. Parch, town engineer for Patamoke, says now that he's okayed Dewey, Cheetum, and Howe to install the new septic system, he can buy that new Bronco and take that trip to Cancun he couldn't afford before. His neighbors at the Shallow Shores Doublewide Park are all agog over his new above ground pool, too.

"We were very pleased to reach an understanding with Mr. Parch. No one can say that he's not willing to negotiate," said Louis B. Cheetum.

Venus Tutweiler, Recording Secretary of the Oysterback Town Commission, has been going through some of the old town ordinances. She has turned up some doozies. In 1796, French could be spoken only between the hours of 3

(See Politics p. 2)

(Politics from p. 1)

p.m. and 1 a.m.; in 1871, it became illegal for anyone to shave on the street on Sundays; in 1923, you could be fined $5 for cleaning fish at the town dock and not cleaning up after yourself. Her favorite, she says, is the 1969 order forbidding the anonymous depositing of tomatoes, cucumbers, zucchini, and bluefish on the steps of town residents' dwellings, businesses, and boats. Many "old timers" will remember 1969 as a year of bumper crops of all of the above.

Devanau County Commissioners voted 3-2, Councilperson Mavis Owerbury abstaining, to accept the federal moneys for improving and adding bicycle lanes to county roads. At their regular Wednesday night meeting, they interpreted "improvements" as digging wider and deeper ditches alongside the roads in question. Council president Fundy LaRue is talking to the science guys at the Wallopsville Lab about breeding bigger and better species of lycra-eating carp with which to stock the proposed trenches.

There was a big flap last week when Chuckles the Albino Clown jumped off the Bay Bridge after being denied tenure at Santimoke College. Chuckles La Rossa was the first Eva Gabor Endowed Chair in Entertainment Studies to suicide off the westbound span.

Chuckles' tenure had been denied by the Faculty Review Committee. They said billing himself as The Albino Clown was politically incorrect. They wanted him to use Pigmentally Impaired.

Based on tapes provided by the Bridge Authority, Chuckles has received a posthumous grant from the Maryland State Arts Council for performance art.

A proposal to charter a town government for Tubman's Corners was struck down again, local voters overwhelmingly coming out against the idea. Citizens Against Charter organizer Dontay Hicks explained, "Not only don't we feel we need the tax burden, but Tubman's Corners is so small, we'd need to rent a town drunk."

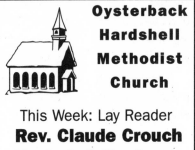

VISIONARY

"Now you take Pat Robertson. He say the Lord speaks to him. He speaks to Oral Roberts. He even communicates with that weasely lookin' Swaggart character," Reverend Claude Crouch, the Traveling Evangelist, growls. "So why shouldn't He speak to me?"

Behind his black-frame glasses, his colorless eyes snap with frustration. His callused fingers play up and down the handle of his chainsaw and his breath hangs on the frosty air like an unfinished thought. "It ain't like I'm not listenin'."

"I don't know," answers Duc Tran Swann, fiddling with her camcorder. She holds it up to her eye, safe behind the lens. "Why do you think God isn't speaking to you?" She pans the camera toward the huge wooden sculpture just behind the Reverend's shoulder so that all of it is captured in the frame. From the top of its head to the tip of its toes, the thing must be about seven feet tall, hewn from a solid log of white pine. To Duc Tran's artist's eye, it looks like Godzilla with wings. Maybe it is Godzilla with wings.

The camcorder hums. She waits patiently, still peering at the old preacher through the camera's eye. Behind him, crows settle on the empty branches of the sycamore tree.

"It ain't like I'm not ready, willing, and able to wear the Gospel armor," Reverend Crouch frets. "Now, I'm not sayin' the Lord don't speak to me, mind you. It's just that he speaks to me in a different way." He turns and pats the knee of the sculpture. "It was the Lord who told me to go out and start makin' these here statchoos," he

confides. With a sweep of his hand, he indicates the wooden carvings spread out on the gravel around the Gospelmobile, the battered white Econoline Van that serves as his home and his studio. Today it is parked in the lot at the Blue Crab Tavern. Somehow, it fits right in among the pickup trucks and lead sleds of the regular patrons.

Duc Tran swings the camera around to give a good view of the chainsawed sculpture display. Giant crabs, crosses hung with garlands of flowers, a weeping Madonna, a howling coyote, a thing that is either an angel or a vulture. All of them are painted in eye-blinding neon colors laid on from spray cans.

"Now," Reverend Crouch continues with a crafty smile, "if I was to tell you that God told me to take up a chain saw and carve up alla these things, you'd say I was crazy, wouldn't you?"

"No, I wouldn't say that," Duc Tran replies from behind the camera. She zooms tightly in on the Madonna's face. The tears are glued-on sequins. The Madonna's expression is dyspeptic. So is the coyote's. So is Reverend Crouch's, as if too many years of fast food on Route 13 between Oysterback and Virginia Beach have taken their toll on the evangelistic digestion.

"A lotta people would, so's I don't tell 'em," Reverend Crouch tells the camera. "But it's true. God told me to carve them statchoos, so I done it."

He takes a Frito from the bag in his lap and chews it thoughtfully as the camera watches.

"I take all my guidance from the Lord. When he said, 'Claude, shut down The True Doctrine Transmission Shop and quit shifting gears for God on the sawdust trail,' I said, 'I hear You, Lord!' And, when he said, 'Claude, them Condos for Christ you sellin' in Wenona's all gonna blow over in that hurricane,' I listened. So, when the Lord said, 'Claude, put down that Treemaster 4100 and take up the forty-eight-inch Lumberjack All Pro,' that's just what I done. And I think it shows, don't you? I'm getting a cleaner line and a better grain. You got to trust the Lord when it comes to carvin' out something like this statchoo of Jesus here."

"Uh-huh," Duc Tran murmurs. It still looks like Godzilla to her, but she doesn't say so.

"No, I'm not crazy," the Traveling Evangelist says proudly. "I'm a visionary. Innit that the word you used?" He glares at the camera.

"Visionary," Duc Tran repeats. "A visionary artist."

"It's a gift from God," Claude asserts piously. "Of course, alla these here statchoos is for sale. You be sure to put that part in. Doin' the Lord's chainsawing costs money. I got overheads," he adds darkly.

"Okay," Duc Tran says. She flips a switch and the camcorder stops running.

Claude blinks once or twice behind his glasses then stands up on shaky knees. He cocks his head, as if listening, then nods. "Yes, Lord! I will!" he says, and starts up the chain saw. The machine's growl cuts across the hard, cold winter air. "Gotta get back to work now," he shouts over the noise. "The Lord wants a little more foreshadowing and perspective on Jesus." He swings the grinding chainsaw toward the big carving behind him, grimacing.

"The Lord says it looks too much like Godzilla," he shouts as he lays into the raw wood.

☺OYSTERBACK BUGEYE

| Helga Wallop, Editor | PO Box 3, Oysterback MD 21000 | 25 cents |

🦀 Published every now and then or whenever there's news... 🦀

oysterback.com

Virtual Ferrus Better than Real Thing

The Dislocated Waterman Retraining Program over at the Community College is really working. Hudson Swann and Junior Redmond have used their newly acquired computer skills to hack into the FBI's secret files on everyone in the West Hundred. If you want to see yours, stop by Junie's workshop in the evenings. Bring your own printer paper.

In related news, Ferrus T. Buckett, the world's oldest waterman, who is somewhere between 70 and death, now has his own web site. You can reach him at http://www.curmudgeon.com.

Speaking of cranky old white guys, Eurydice Chew reports from Bethel Branch that Hurricane Bertha caused a big leak in the shape of Arnold Toynbee to appear on the wall of her family room. Since she is a registered Independent, she says she fails to understand why this happened to her, but the curious have come from as far away as the former Soviet Union to view the apparition, leaving offerings of Wonderbread, homemade Pink Floyd tapes, and sympathetic magic items having something to do with Bob Dole's piles, or at least that's what someone told her. Eurydice says she enjoys the company, as long as they don't show up during her afternoon stories on TV.

Due to the severe shortage of crabs this summer, the Wallopsville Volunteer Fire and Rescue Company has changed the menu for their August 24 fund-raiser. The Chicken Necker Fiesta kicks off at noon with a Bull Lips Bar-B-Que, so come on down.

Racine Boudine, musical director of the West Hundred Community Orchestra, will be guest conductor of the Patamoke Karaoke Chorale over to the Community Theatre In the Oblong Saturday Night. Featured soloist will be Francine Boudine, whose vocal stylings have been heard as far away as the Peach Bottom Moonlite Bay Supper Club in Conowingo, although she lives in Tubman's Corners. She will be backed up by her cousins Gineen, Earlene, and Martine. The Boudines will wear matching peach gowns with sheer overlays trimmed with rhinestone ribbing, provided by Jodi's Fashion Whirl Boutique, except for Racine, who will wear a white tie. The Boudines will be known to many in this region as the former snake-handling gospel quartet.

Oder Bowley, 38, of 4402 Suicide Chicken Road, was arrested by Sheriff Wesley Briscoe and charged with running a farm chop shop and selling stolen agricultural equipment parts roughly the size of your average fast-food joint to unsuspecting farmers in West Virginia.

Madam Zorlina, the Palm Reader out on Route 50, says that Smollet Bowley, brother of Oder, is so stupid, when he

(See Bugeye p. 2)

(Bugeye from p. 1)

comes in, she charges only half price to read his mind.

Omar Hinton wants the whole West Hundred to know that the souvenir items he has ordered from the novelty company in New Jersey have finally arrived. If anyone wants a license plate that says I BRAKE FOR BOONE BROS; a lovely varnished cedar plaque with a decal of the Last Supper that says OYSTERBACK, MARYLAND; a tasteful plastic mug with the Patamoke town seal; or a collection of attractive and useful postcards featuring scenes of the Route 50 Bypass around Wallopsville, drop by the store. Omar says the new ice cream flavor, Lasagna Mint Ripple, has arrived and is available in the freezer case.

Mr. Earl's Party Farm announces that this year's Battle of the Bands will be held in Tonto Rainbird's back pasture after the Reverse Gear Mud Bogs on the 17th. Norris Peavine of Mello Groove D.J. Party Services of Tubman's Corners will emcee the event. Bellicose bands with an attitude, tanned, rested, and out of rehab in time to rock and roll that night will include Albert and the Nasal Hairs, Ginko Revenge, Young

Republicans for Satan, Toadfish Tramps, and Delmar P.'s E-Z Tone Accordianaires performing their hit, "The Jesus Loves Me Polka."

Delbert Runch asks what's yellow and sleeps eight? His answer, a DOT highway truck, always gets laughs from the boys over at the state maintenance barn, especially during pothole repair season.

Over to Slaughter's Crossroads, Floxie Hightower reports that she is channeling Admiral Elmo Zumwalt via a celadon lamp she picked up at a yard sale over to Rhodesdale last spring. The admiral told her that the best place to fish for croakers is out on Irritable Shoal by the 13B can. Floxie and husband Tut hauled in a dozen good-sized hardheads out there Tuesday night with bloodworms, but they're fallen off somewhat this week when the moon changed. Floxie says the Admiral is talking about a good run of red drum this fall, however. Stay tuned, fishermen.

The First Church of Elvis over to Slaughter's Crossroads will be holding a Fried-Lard-Banana-Peanut-Butter Sandwich and Rummage Sale on the 31st. They hope to raise enough money to buy the governor a personality.

Norris and Chickadee Peavine are celebrating the birth of a son. Ross Keanau Brad Peavine, 8 lbs.,10 oz., arrived prematurely while they were honeymooning at Captain and Mrs. Lennie Skinner's rental cottage in Ocean City last week.

Desiree Grinch, proprietor of the Blue Crab Tavern, has announced that she has finally blurred the line between life and performance art. She is applying for a grant from the Jesse Helms Philistine Foundation to take it on the road.

THE CRAB BAIT KILLER

*T*he orange and black crepe paper streamers flap in the chill night air. The flame inside the jack-o'-lantern is guttering down, making its stretched grin look mean and sinister. It's as if old Jack sees something that you don't, those triangular eyes shifting this way and that with each spurt of the flame. That skeleton in the community center doorway is only paper, isn't it? It's a trick of the breeze, the way those bones dance and beckon to you. It's as if it's talking to that ghost hanging in the tree, the one that's supposed to be a sheet, but now with the mist rising, it looks kind of real, like a spirit walking.

The littlest trick-or-treaters, so full of sugar-powered energy and mischief a couple of hours ago, are now collapsed in drowsy heaps. Former mermaids and Power Rangers and pirates and little princesses sleep open-mouthed in daddy's arms, being taken home to bed and The Mummy, who was running the apple dunk, has taken off his bandages to become a yawning Wimsey Jump, algebra teacher with classes tomorrow.

An angel and a vampire are pushing wide old brooms around, making little piles of glitter and candy corn and paper cups on the empty floor, but Delmar P.'s Accordionaires have packed up and gone, along with several witches, a goblin, Elvis, and a duck blind that won first prize for best costume. The Haunted Hayride is parked by the doorway, just an old farm trailer with some bales of straw.

Outside, under the yellow-leafed trees, a gang of kids, too old for this baby stuff with the costumes and candy, but not too old to come down to the community center to see what's happening, has congregated in the darkness, and the mood is on them to plot some harm, orange ends of cigarettes glowing in the dark, the hiss of a contraband beer can being opened. Not really bad kids, you understand, just too many slasher movies and hopping hormones and too little parental supervision. Still, they jump a little when the voice comes out of the darkness.

"Some night, huh?"

It's Junie Redmond, hidden inside the rubber head of his Cryptkeeper costume, sitting on the fence in the darkness. They don't know how long he's been there, or what he's heard, but they sort of try to hide the beer cans. "Yeah," Junie continues casually, crushing out his own cigarette against the sole of his boot. "Some night. You know, it's nights like this when the Crab Bait Killer walks."

"Oh yeah," Huddie Swann says, and it's like he's suddenly appeared in the darkness, standing over there under the old oak, but you understand, these are cool kinds, not afraid of anything, and they just stare sullenly. "The Crab Bait Killer," Huddie says with relish, enjoying the sound of the words. "It was a night like this when we seen him, wannit, Junie?"

"Oh, yeah. It was back with them Harbeson boys. Levin and Daniel. They lived in that old shack back down there in the marsh." Even though no one wants to, they all look down the marsh, where the weatherbeaten frame of an old shanty leans crazily toward the water, gaping windows like empty eye sockets in the moonlight.

"Lived out on that old marsh, just the two of them. Crazy old men. One cold night, just like this, Levin had a big fight with Daniel. Took an old tonghead and stove in the back of Daniel's head," Junie says conversationally. "Just like you'd smash a pumpkin."

"And then, Levin took Daniel and chopped him all up and salted him down for crab bait," Huddie adds. "Used him all up on his trotlines."

"He baited up real good," Junie sighs. "Levin caught lots a crabs off ole Daniel that fall. Especially with his fingers and toes."

"Then one night, Levin was sittin' all alone down in the shanty, and he hears something comin' up outta the water."

From the river, there is the sound of a splash. It is probably just a bluefish, but a couple of kids jump.

"And he heard something that sounded like a person creeping up on the marsh." Just then the wind rustles across the grass. "And something rattled at the shanty door latch. Levin opened the door. It was Daniel, come back!"

"He was all black and shapeless and nasty, makin' this weird noise. He come back to get Levin."

One of the tougher boys mutters an obscenity beneath his breath, but everyone else stands stock still as a light seems to flicker back and forth in the empty windows of the shanty.

Of course, it is just a trick of the water and the moon.

Isn't it?

"Junie, you see that?" Huddie asks, horrified. "You see that light?"

"Oh, m'gawd! I think Daniel's walking again!" Junie cries.

A dark, limpy figure emerges from the shack, slowly shambling up through the marshes toward the community center. It's sort of limping and awkward, like it's been dead and come back from beneath the water.

"It's coming this way!" Junie cries.

"Run!" Huddie shrieks. One girl gives a little squeal, and two of the younger ones cut and run right there. The big ones stand their ground.

At least until the thing in the marsh gives a shriek. It's a high, unearthly wail, a sound that cuts through the night and right into your bone and blood. The dark shapeless shape keeps on coming though, right toward them. It shrieks again, a sound like souls in hell.

Then you see kids scatter in all directions. Gone, just like that. Not of course, that anyone actually believes this stuff, but hey, it's time to get out of here and go home where it's safe.

Junie lights another cigarette, the flame casting his face into an eerie relief. He and Huddie don't move, but watch the thing approach them until the lights from the building fall across it.

"Works every time," Delmar P. says, folding his accordion against his chest. "Worked on us twenty years ago; works now."

"Not only that, they left their beer," Junie says, handing cans to Delmar P. and Huddie. "Still nice and cold."

"Here's to the Crab Bait Killer," Huddie says, lifting his beer.

Far off, down on the marsh, a small, lonely wind laments across the empty grass.

MISS NETTIE IN DURANCE VILE

$\mathcal{A}$ long with everyone else in Oysterback, I, Desiree Grinch, proprietor of the Blue Crab Tavern, could cheerfully lynch Deputy Johnny Ray Insley. Can you imagine hauling a nice lady like Miss Nettie Leery off to jail for picking a few crabs in her kitchen?

Chief and Mrs. Briscoe took their week's vacation at Captain and Mrs. Lennie Skinner's rental cottage in Ocean City, leaving that damn fool Deputy Johnny Ray Insley in charge. So we knew we could count on Johnny Ray doing something stupid as he does every year. But we were not amused when he arrested Miss Nettie Leery for picking crabs in her own kitchen because someone told him it is against some shinybutt bureaucrat law.

Now, I do not care what someone has to say. There are lots of Miss Nettie type ladies who supplement their Social Security and their late husband Alva's railroad pension by picking crabs in their kitchens for a few much needed extra dollars a week. I am here to tell you that I would not be afraid to eat off the floor in Miss Nettie Leery's kitchen, she's that trim a housekeeper. And I have been using her crab meat at the Blue Crab Tavern (★★★ *Guide Michelin*) for years without anyone dying of anything but bliss over my Blue Crab Imperial.

But I am also here to tell you that I have heard certain seafood people like Litey Clash sit at my bar and brag about how they import crabmeat from countries where *E. Coli* is the national bird. Frankly, I would have serious questions about crab meat Amnesty International has listed as a torture device. *And that is legal.* But a lady like Miss

Nettie picking a few pounds of crabs in her kitchen is against the law? I ask you.

But the minute Chief Briscoe left, Johnny Ray Insley takes it into his little pointy head that Miss Nettie's a dangerous criminal for picking crab meat in her own kitchen. He bursts into her mudroom, .38 at the ready, and arrests her for illegal picking. Miss Nettie is still in her apron with her hair rollers up under the net for her canasta game that night, and he's got her in shackles like she's Alonzo Deaver gone off with the Uzi again.

When I got down to the jail, Johnny Ray had Miss Nettie locked up in a cell, and I like to have blistered the paint right off the walls. I was using words I did not ordinarily use when I am not talking trash at second base, and I think by then Johnny Ray knew he had made a serious mistake, but he wasn't about to back down, just because he is so bloody minded. So I just sat down and told him I had a mind to bar him from the Blue Crab for the next three lifetimes and I was not moving until he let poor Miss Nettie out of the lock-up. Then I started calling up everyone on the station phone, daring that jellyfish to stop me. He would have tried too, but then Omar Hinton came in, waving his price gun around, and stared him down. Omar's had it in for Johnny Ray since he tried to close down the old men's spades game down to the store as illegal gambling.

Doreen and Jeanne threw their kids into Doreen's Cherokee and headed off to Annapolis to pry our state delegate Orville Orvall off his permanent bar stool at McGarvey's. Junior went after P.B.J. Haddaway, everyone's favorite courthouse barnacle, and Hudson took off in search of Judge Findlay Fish, who is known to be extremely partial to Miss Nettie's crabcakes. Hagar closed up the P.O., and she and Helga came over and joined me in the sit-in. We just sat there and glared at Johnny Ray. Then Wimsey and Professor Shepherd came in, and Professor Shepherd started a long discourse on civil disobedience and how in Oysterback, people do what they damn well please as long as they don't do it in the street and scare the dogs.

I guess by the time Poot Wallop arrived with a bushel of crabs and several picking knives and we all started to pick crabmeat over Johnny Ray, he was beginning to get the bigger picture. Still, I had to enjoy the way Miss Carlotta Hackett and Mrs. Reverend Briscoe roared up that pink Cadillac and prayed long and loud for Johnny Ray's soul, and Reverend Briscoe led us all in many, many choruses of "We Shall Overcome," which some of us have not sung since the '60s. Crystal Tiffany tap danced on Johnny Ray's feet and told him they were through as a couple. Beth Redmond recited "Give Me Liberty or Give Me Death." It was very moving, except Little Olivier started crying in the middle of it and she had to change him on Johnny Ray's desk. You really had to hand it to Wade and Mookie, though. They just sat there and cleaned their teeth with their big old Buck knives. By then, the word was out over to Wallopsville and Patamoke. Tonto Rainbird came in and announced he was holding a Reverse Gear Pickup Truck Race Benefit Mud Bog For The Miss Nettie Defense Fund. Sister Gibbs brought in a file hidden in a Jell-O mold.

It was quite a crowd down there at the town hall when the media (Tom Horton) came by to write it all up for the *Sun*. I have to admit that by that time, some people had nearly forgotten all about poor Miss Nettie back there in durance vile.

Then Judge Fish came in and read Johnny Ray the riot act, calling him twenty kinds of an interfering idiot and demanding Miss Nettie's release. But Miss Nettie was long gone. There was just an empty cell and all her hair rollers all over.

While we were all carrying on out front, wouldn't you know that the Boone Bros would take matters into their own hands? They just backed up to Miss Nettie's cell, threw a log chain around the bars, attached the other end to the We Fix truck, put it into gear, and pulled that window right out. Then they lifted Miss Nettie, as gentle as a pair of doves, out of that cell and spirited her away to some secret place known only to Gabe and Mike.

Well, Chief Briscoe came back and straightened everything out, and Johnny Ray is banned for the next five lifetimes from the Blue

Crab. Miss Nettie came back last night, looking tanned and refreshed and ten years younger. I put crab back on the menu again, and things are about as back to normal as they ever are in Oysterback.

Miss Nettie won't tell us where the Boone Bros took her while she was on the lam, but she says it was out of this world.

THANKFUL FOR THE MEAT

*R*alph, the youngest Boone Brother, has returned to Oysterback for Thanksgiving. Not so much because he wants to, either. Would you want to visit your family if they ran the Boone Bros We Fix & Road Kill Cooked Here Cafe and Garage? Well, actually his older brothers Gabe and Mike are all the family he has, and he finds them embarrassing, if you want to know the truth. They're these burned-out old hippies who haven't quite figured out the '60s are over, and have been over for quite a while, too, Ralph thinks contemptuously. The '80s were more his decade, when greed was a good thing. What went wrong?

Actually, Ralph doesn't have much choice about coming back to town. For the past couple of years, he's been in Jupiter, Florida, but since the Special Investigations Unit began asking a lot of questions and about the same time, his fourth wife, Cyndee, left him for that pit boss she met in Vegas....

Well, coming home for a nice long visit seems to be a wise thing to do; he should be thankful this hick dump hasn't dried up and blown away. Oysterback is about the last place on the face of the earth anyone would look for him, especially Monte "Big Tuna" D'Abrunzio, who is someone you and I don't want to know about.

In Oysterback, Ralph is explained as a change-of-life baby.

Miss Catherine Swann dreads Thanksgiving, because that's the day that Mr. Hardee gears up for the Christmas light season, and all seven-hundred thousand of his string lights have to come out of storage and be tested, strand by strand, before he can start putting them up all over the outside of the house the day after. Imagine if you will, lines of Christmas lights strung out everywhere, all around the house, while Hardee goes over them, bulb by bulb, looking for the one burnt out light that will keep the whole chain from lighting up most of Devanau County for the holiday season. There are strands of multi-colored lights draped over every surface in the house, up and down the stairs, around the living and dining room, through the hallway to the kitchen, around the corner and out the door. She's terrified if Hardee doesn't trip over the cords and break a leg, he'll fall off the roof mounting the "Nona Classic Life-Size Santa" and "Eight Reindeer & Rudolph" and kill himself. You try cooking a turkey under those conditions.

She and Mr. Hardee are going to eat their Thanksgiving dinner at the Ye Old Colonial Watershed Bed and Breakfast Inn, if she can drag him away from his latest acquisition that long. Mr. Hardee has added a state of the art "Comp-U-Lite Talking Scrooge with Tiny Tim" to his thirty-seven secular and fourteen religious life-size illuminated holiday lawn figures, which includes the legendary and much-coveted "Good Shepherd of Graceland Elvis Figure" that has made him the envy of other Christmas Lighters throughout the tri-state area. For this, Mr. Hardee is very thankful. Before Miss Catherine can examine what she's thankful for, she hears a horrible crash and the sound of thousands of tiny plastic lights breaking.

After lurking fruitlessly in Faraday Hicks' wood lot over to Slaughter's Crossroads for several weekends, precariously balanced for endless hours on a tiny stand, sitting dead still through rain, sleet, heat, and a couple of hard frosts, Junie Redmond, whose greatest Thanksgiving wish has been a deer to fill the freezer, has given up all hope. Looks like the family will be eating a lot of tuna noodle casserole and Hamburger Helper this winter.

On Junie's way back to Oysterback, an eighteen-point buck hurtles out of the woods just past Tubman's Corners and slams into the side of his truck. Mercifully, the deer is killed on impact, but Junie, a man who knows how to appreciate irony, is thankful for the meat.

Little known facts about well-known people are always useful to have to hand. Desiree Grinch, who knows which buttons to push and where quite a few bodies are buried, has begged, borrowed, and blackmailed three twenty-pound turkeys from various and sundry sinners around Devanau County, and is roasting them up in the kitchen at the Blue Crab Tavern. While they are in the oven, she and Professor Shepherd are whipping up thirty pounds of mashed potatoes to go with the two hundred yeast rolls and three gallons of stringbean casserole they've already put together and stored in the freezer. When the turkeys are done to a golden brown, Desiree and the professor will load them into her monster truck and take the whole deal over to A Safe Place, the women's shelter in Patamoke. Desiree Grinch is a woman who also knows a thing or two about being poor and in trouble. She's thankful she's still capable of moral ambiguity in a good cause.

Over to Miss Nettie Leery's, delicious smells drift through the house along with that ineffable air of tension that happens whenever Hudson Swann and Buddy Leery are in the same room for too long. Fortunately, they can focus their attention on the Macy's Thanksgiving Day Parade, rather than try to make polite conversation. Both have been warned about opening their mouths about politics and starting something. Miss Nettie and Jeanne are in the kitchen, and Jeanne is lecturing her mother about the evils of cholesterol as she layers the sweet potatoes and Marshmallow Fluff into a baking dish. The twins, Ashley and Amber, are upstairs, having found their mother's high school yearbook in her girlhood room. Jeanne, who thought that Farrah Fawcett hairdo was quite glamorous back there in the '70s, would be horrified to know how hilarious her daughters find her prom photos.

The kit-kat clock slowly ticks away the minutes until dinnertime. Some meal, Miss Nettie thinks. A week to prepare it and fifteen minutes to eat it. She is thankful that she and Miss Sister Gibbs have booked themselves on that Caribbean Christmas Cruise because if she has to cook another holiday meal for this family, she'll scream. Although, being Miss Nettie, she would never actually think that.

She'll just let them turn up Christmas day and be surprised.

Down on Black Dog Road, Ferrus T. Buckett, the world's oldest waterman and carver of genuine reproduction antique decoys, has forsworn the traditional turkey in favor of a little something he found in Julia Child. His guest, the Mozart soprano Aurora Beauchamp, opens the Veuve Cliquot just as the fruits des mer vol-au-vents are ready to come out of the oven. Ferrus is thankful that the morelles are suitably fresh, and the Chambord soufflé has risen properly.

Over to Patamoke Seafood, Venus Tutweiler shuts down her fork-lift just as the microwave timer in the lunchroom starts to ping.

With a sigh, she sinks into a chair and removes the cellophane from her Lean Cuisine Turkey Dinner. As she waits for the gravy to cool down, she pops the tab on a Caffeine Free Diet Pepsi. Venus hoists the can in a toast to the silent factory. "Here's to Thanksgiving," she proclaims. She's thankful she's drawn a holiday shift. "It's a dysfunctional family reunion where everyone brings a covered dish and an unresolved issue."

Nonetheless, when the mouse, who lives behind the refrigerator, pokes its head out, she's careful to drop a bit of stuffing on the floor within the rodent's reach.

Sometimes, even Venus hates to eat alone.

SLOW DANCING WITH THE ANGEL OF DEATH DOWN TO BUDDY'S BAR AND GRILL

Pay no attention to the man behind the curtain. He may be afraid, but *I'm* not.

There is a time, dear Desiree, in *everyone's* life when they should get drunk with a friend and tell *all*. We're working on that tonight. You see? I told you those weekend people wouldn't be here; they never are, and besides, tonight, this isn't their dock, it's Buddy's Bar and Grill. That's why I'm hanging these chili pepper lights and handing you this bottle of Tres Brujos Tequila, my dear. The bar is officially open. Of course, a bar's got to have some music. There, now Patsy Kline's singing a somebody-done-me-wrong song. Buddy's Bar and Grill is the sort of place where somebody-done-me-wrong songs are the *only* music they play, even when they're sung by Cecilia Bartolli, who comes up next? She's fabulous, you'll love her. We went to hear her in Milan, right before Julian got too sick to travel.

And now, I've come home to die, just another tired old queen whose HIV went into AIDS overdrive. Dead at twenty-eight, twenty-nine if I'm lucky. But it's been one hell of a life, you know. I've had everything I ever wanted, done everything I ever wanted to do. And almost *everyone*, too. Don't look at me like that, dear, and for God's sake don't start to cry. No tears at Buddy's Bar and Grill, it's not allowed. Aren't these chili pepper lights a hoot? What do they remind you of? No, *don't* tell me. We'll just leave them here and those weekend people will wonder what the hell happened. Drink up, dear, we need to be richly, gloriously drunk tonight, and Tres Brujos is the only way to go. Confusion to our enemies!

You and I, Desiree, are going to plan my wake. You're the only one I trust to do it, you know. Mom and Jeanne will just tack it all up; they won't be in any shape to do much. They're not handling this very well, and I *must* try to shield them from pain. But you will, Desiree, you're the strong one. Have another drink and a bite of that lime. We drank Tres Brujos every night when we were in Mexico, Julian and I. Have you ever had tequila by moonlight in the *ruinas* at Palenqué? Marvelous. Drink, there's a good girl.

In Manhattan, they called Buddy Leery "Charles," and he worked as a production designer for the movies, but back home, I've *always* been "Buddy." I left here a long time ago, not because I hated it, but because my chances of finding personal fulfillment as a gay artist in Oysterback were pretty slender, unless I wanted to spend the rest of my life doing window display over to Omar Hinton's store.

I have come home, darling Desiree, to die among my own people. All over America, we're coming home. Your children are crawling home to die. Look at the fireflies across the river in the trees. Do you think they're attracted by our chili pepper lights? What would they produce if they mated? I hope wherever I go, Julian's there. God, I miss him so much. Heaven for the climate, hell for the company! Drink up and pass the bottle over here.

I *know* you would like to resign as general manager of the universe, especially when you look at your golden boy and see him dying. The poster boy for those blond Anglo Saxon Protestant Oysterback genes is losing his looks, Miss Desiree. I *used* to be so pretty. Sweet, funny Buddy, who is already starting to blur a little around the edges, like a fading photograph. Maybe death is where you just get smaller and smaller and one day you just aren't there anymore...gone. I *cannot* think about what's ahead, not tonight. Thinking about unpleasant things is forbidden at Buddy's Bar and Grill. *Look* at me, Desiree. I am the Angel of Death. Did you ever think the Angel of Death would be a golden boy with AIDS?

Well, I always did think ninety-nine percent of being gay was good bones. And I'm vain enough to be sort of glad that I'm going while I still have all my hair. By the time I don't, I won't care any more. I'll be beyond all that. That will be very restful. Drink, drink, drink. I want you drunk, so I can be drunk. It doesn't hurt so much when I'm drunk. I had a dream about you. You were chasing me with a bar tab. Naughty girl, Desiree, drink.

See this? It's a sarcoma. One of the first warning signs, you know. Yes, darling Desiree, there *is* something violently obscene about a man not yet thirty planning his own wake. Hand me the bottle, dear, that's good. Try some of that bel paese. Isn't this the most *wonderful* tape? Patsy and Cecilia and Reba and Kirsten and Kitty and Maria. This is the tape I want to have playing then. I picked out all my favorite things. Poor Hudson; my brother-in-law is a lovely man, but he *won't* like this opera music. He'll like Reba though. He and Junie will be pallbearers, of course. We've talked about that. Straight men are *so* funny. They really *don't* get it, but if anyone had *ever* tried to hassle me, you know Huddie and Junie and the boys would tear them a new hole. Because I'm one of Us. An Oysterback native. *Un Bel Di.* Confession: I've always had a tiny crush on Huddie. Don't ever tell him, you *know* what he's like. When he was young, he had the most *beautiful skin*. You're not drinking. That's better, now the lime. Good. Ah, you're laughing. Good girl.

Remember when you came to New York and we went to see *Madame Butterfly*? Afterwards, we went to the Russian Tea Room and I introduced you to Sam Ramey and you giggled just like a little girl? Julian adored you, you know. We *have* had some good times, haven't we? I'm sorry I won't be able to play softball any more. I'll miss that. But I can still watch the games. It's funny; the first part of my life I couldn't wait to leave town, and the last part of it, I wanted only to come home. It means a great deal to me to die among my own people, you know. Not all of these redneck men are as macho as everyone thinks they are, either. Oh, I could tell you *stories*. But I won't. I've *never* been one to kiss and tell. Take it right to the grave with me. Bad joke.

Don't forget the casablanca lilies, now, there must be casablanca lilies, and you have to get Johnny Ray to sing "A Trumpet Shall Sound" just like he does every Christmas when they do *The Messiah*. And we shall be changed. No, no, it was just that a goose ran over my grave. Don't forget to notify everyone in New York, some of them will want to come. The ones who are left. It's nature's way of thinning the herd.

No, I'm fine, really. Drink, my dear. Drink up. Good girl. Smell that honeysuckle? Isn't that divine? Oh, there's Patsy again. Come on, Desiree, stagger to your feet, darling girl, and dance with me. A slow dance with the Angel of Death down here at Buddy's Bar and Grill. God, yes I am drunk. Very drunk. And so are you, my dear. So come and dance with the Angel of Death. We'll dance by the light of the chili pepper lights to a somebody-done-me-wrong song, here at Buddy's Bar and Grill.

Promise me that this is the way you will remember me, your friend, the beautiful and young Angel of Death, slow dancing at Buddy's Bar and Grill, the two of us drunk as two skunks on a hot summer night, laughing. Are those your tears or mine?

Winter

CABIN FEVER

*T*here was a big snowstorm last week, and it was a while before the plows got down to Oysterback, so most people were stuck at home for a couple of days. Worse, the cable went down and stayed down for almost a week.

Without their electronic babysitter, most people were getting pretty squirrely by the end of the first day. By the second day, if Satan had come around Oysterback with a satellite dish, even Reverend Briscoe might have at least listened to his sales pitch.

When you live this far back up the marsh, it's hard to get any kind of TV reception at all. Especially at my place, since Professor Shepherd took the .12 gauge and blew out the Magnavox over the bar when that snollygoster Newt Gingrich put his piggy little face on CNN once too often.

Now, I, Desiree Grinch, proprietor of the Blue Crab Tavern, have inner resources that I am able to fall back on when I'm snowed in and the cable goes down. I occupied my time by reading my way through the works of Anthony Trollope and experimenting with different hair colors. By the second day, I was Sunflower Terra Cotta blonde, halfway through *The Eustace Diamonds* and contemplating Sorrel Toast and *Barchester Towers* if I didn't kill Earl Don first.

Did you ever notice that men don't know how to be sick? Every five minutes they need a glass of orange juice or their pillows fluffed up or you to call 911 because they felt a twinge. A woman can be dying and she'll get out of bed and go to work, but let a man get the sniffles and all hell breaks loose. Finally, I went downstairs and opened the bar, just to get away from him. Even if no one came in, I would be out of earshot of Earl Don and his deathbed need for me to fetch him a Kleenex not two feet away from his hand. Without TV, he was as lost as a pig in a peach orchard and twice as much trouble, especially with a head cold.

As you can tell, not everyone around here is capable of entertaining themselves in such a productive fashion as I. Once some people lose their TV, they tend to get a real bad case of the whim-whams, if you know what I mean and I think you do. So when people started to trickle into the Blue Crab late that afternoon, even though the roads were still bad, I wasn't much surprised.

"Colder and partly cloudy," Huddie recited when he came up from the harbor to grab a cup of hot coffee. "I went into such bad withdrawal without those *Simpsons* re-runs that I actually had to go outside and shovel two feet of 'partly cloudy' out of my boat."

If that weren't enough, he said his mother-in-law Miss Nettie went so stir crazy she went out and chain-sawed up that old tree that fell down in the yard when Huddie and Junie Redmond backed into it with their motorized Port-O-San duck blind (patent pending) when they were trying to get her old antenna set back up again so she wouldn't miss *One Life to Live*.

Just about then, Doreen Redmond came in, carrying a bad case of kid overload. She didn't even notice my new hair color, which you would think she would, being a professional, and not one to be selfish with her opinions. "My Gawd," she said, "Junie woke up this morning, turned on the TV, and said, 'The cable still isn't back up; if it doesn't come back up soon, we might actually have to talk to each other.' He's in the kitchen tryin' to cook something with that bluefish that's been in the deep freeze since last summer." She shuddered. "I told the kids that I had to come down to the Curl Up 'n' Dye because I had to make sure that the pipes weren't gonna freeze up, but I just *had* to get out of there. If Jason plays that damn Bob Dylan CD one more time, I might have to call over to The Towers in Cambridge and reserve a room for myself. Why can't these kids get their own music instead of playin' ours all over again?"

"If you can remember the '60s, you probably weren't there," Huddie said to the deer head over the pool table and laughed a hollow laugh that turned into a strangled sob. "What'm I gonna do without my football?" he cried, and put his head down on the bar, his emotions just all tore up. "I dreamed last night that Mike Ditka's hair had its own pre-game show!"

"I need my cable and I need it now!" It was just too much for Doreen; she broke down too, and I knew I was going to be close to the edge if something didn't happen soon. There's only so much a person can take. We looked at each other; then we did the only thing we knew how to do under these circumstances.

The sunset was streaming through the window, the color of warm beaches in Miami, when Earl Don shuffled his way downstairs in his

good shepherd bathrobe and his sheepskin slippers, pitifully asking if we were out of cold tablets. He found us all sprawled on the pool table in the last shaft of sunlight, huddled against the coming night, lifting our feeble voices against the forces of darkness and the decline of civilization.

We'd worked our way through the lyrics to "Gilligan's Island," "The Flintstones," "I Love Lucy," "Happy Trails," "That Girl," "Secret Agent," and "Rawhide." Now we were working on our three part harmony for "The Brady Bunch" and hotly debating the Patty Duke question. Was it Patty or Cathy? Were they "cous-ins, unbearable cous-ins" or "cous-ins, identical cou-sins?"

Cabin fever is a terrible thing, that's all I've got to say.

MALE BONDING

*P*arsons Dreedle has been having a religious revival lately; he had a bad scare with his last prostate examination with Dr. Wheedleton, and it has given him reason to think about things he has not previously considered, like God. Although, you might think that owning a funeral home and being around death all the time would make him think about God before this, which maybe he has and no one noticed it before.

But even Reverend Briscoe, who is a nice man, was nonplussed when Parsons stood up during the offering last Sunday and announced that he could see the ghost of Bunky Redmond floating in the back of the church, smiling at him because he, Parsons, had made a personal commitment to Jesus. "I can see him just as clear as day," Parsons said dramatically, pointing to a space somewhere around the stained glass window of the Miracle of the Loaves and Fishes that was donated by Busbee Clinton, who owns the seafood plant. "He's so happy that I have accepted Jesus as my personal savior."

In spite of its name, Oysterback Hardshell Methodist Church is pretty softshell; we don't go in for purple-haired preachers screaming about the fires of hell and smirking about how they're going to heaven and you're not. So you can just imagine what people were thinking when Parsons interrupted the service to make this announcement. Everyone was certainly looking, even little Miss Buck, the organist, whose fingers kept playing "Jesus, Savior, Pilot

Me," as she peered over her glasses, mouth agape, at Parsons, standing up in the second pew, his hair standing up all over his head, pointing toward the back of the church like the statue of our Glorious War Dead over to the courthouse at the county seat.

"I wish I could get those kind of theatrics out of him when he's trying out for *Mame*," Hagar Jump murmured to her husband Wimsey, who was as startled as little Miss Buck.

Desiree Grinch snorted, and had to put her hymnal up over her face, but Earl Don, who was passing the collection plate on the other side of the church, almost dropped it. Hudson Swann turned and looked, just to be sure that old Bunk wasn't back there. Which was what most people did; people in Oysterback don't see things like that, or if they do, they keep it to themselves. Miss Nettie Leery didn't say anything, but she didn't have to; her disapproval was so manifest you could have reached out and touched it with your hand. St. Paul tells us not to cut the fool, especially in church, and she takes those words to heart. "If you want to make a scene, wait for the revival to come through" is her motto.

"He's smiling because he's so happy that I've come home to the Lord," Parsons cried, his face all alight, his finger pointing to a place near where the stained glass fish pour out of the stained glass basket, with the winter sunlight pouring through. And then he sat down. There was a moment of silence, and then the ushers began passing the collection plates again and everything went on about as usual.

Paisley and Junior Redmond, the late Bunky's sons, were not in church that Sunday; they and their wives, Doreen and Beth, had decided to go down to Captain and Mrs. Lennie Skinner's rental cottage in Ocean City that weekend, since Reba McEntire was at the Civic Center. Besides, Doreen's mother had offered to keep the kids, all of them, and you don't get an offer like that everyday.

But you can bet that the story got back to them by Sunday night, one way or another. It doesn't matter who, or how many who's told them; in a small town like Oysterback, news, especially news that makes someone else look more foolish than the rest of us, travels as fast as a crab on a hot plank.

Monday night at half-time, the Redmond brothers were over at Junie's, in the den, and it was Paisley who brought up the subject, him being younger. Doreen was upstairs supervising the two younger ones' teeth brushing; Chelsea was on the phone in the kitchen, microwaving popcorn; and Jason was lost in some seventeen-year-old interior space involving his Game Boy. The entire conversation between the Redmond brothers went like this:

"Personally, I can't see Daddy doin' anything like that. He only went to church Christmas and Easter," Paisley said, reaching for a handful of potato chips from the bag on the coffee table.

"You can say that again," Junie said, popping another can of beer. "Daddy wasn't one to make a big show, ever."

"I can't even remember him even thinking about Parsons." Paisley put his feet on the ottoman and slowly worked off his shoes. Being in the auto body repair business he's on his feet all day, and sometimes they hurt him at night.

"Daddy would think that anything that was going on between Parsons and Jesus wasn't any of his business," Junie pointed out. He belched a little behind his hand, since Doreen wasn't there to reprimand him.

The game came back on, Chelsea got off the phone, and Jason put down the Game Boy. Doreen came downstairs and settled in on the couch again, commandeering the microwave popcorn.

"It's good to have these kind of talks, you know, between brothers, once in a while," Paisley said at the next commercial break, when dancing disposable razors filled the screen. "Pass the onion dip, willya?"

"Yeah, I feel better, too," Junie said. "Any more of those Cheese Doodles over there?"

Loelia Redmond, who now winters in Florida with her sister Florence, didn't hear about Bunky's manifestation at the church until Easter, and then she had plenty to say to Parsons. After all, she was married to Bunky for forty-two years and knew him better than Parsons Dreedle.

Parsons' religious revival seems to have calmed down quite a bit since Doc Wheedleton told him the test results, but as noted before, Oysterback is a small town. You get out of line once, and you spend the rest of your life listening to the retired watermen and farmers tease you about it down to Omar Hinton's store, embellishing a moment of folly into a full-blown epic. It gets better every time they tell it, too; Omar thinks they ought to sell it to Hollywood.

BARON SAMEDI ON BINGO NIGHT

After Christmas, Miss Florence Redmond, mother of Junior and Paisley, goes to Palmetto Lip, Florida, to stay over the winter with her daughter Donna and her son-in-law Martin, who own a couple of dry cleaning franchises down there. Donna and Marty wouldn't move back up North if you paid them; they have become Floridians through and through.

Miss Florence has been a widow for nearly twenty years, so when she met Baron Samedi at the First Palmetto Protestant Church of Santeria Bingo Night, everyone was just glad that she had met such a nice gentlemen, even if he was Lord of the Graveyard and a god; the Baron, as few in Oysterback knew until recently, is a powerful member of the Afro-Caribbean pantheon who rules over the dead.

Of course, Ferrus T. Buckett knew, but Ferrus, being the world's oldest waterman, somewhere between seventy and death himself, knows everything, or he would have you believe.

Still and all, when the Baron came up to visit Miss Florence and the Oysterback end of the family at the holidays, people were somewhat apprehensive. What do you say to someone who dresses all in black, wears a top hat, and walks around town with the legs and feet of a huge crow? His enormous, splayed talons gingerly carried his skeletal body around our muddy streets, and he supported himself with the help of his silver headed cane, and you could tell he was a little uncomfortable with the wetlands, so different from the tropical jungles where he lives. It was the first time Baron Samedi had been up this way before, and he shivered slightly in the damp Chesapeake cold, this mahogany colored, somber gentleman with the glowing red eyes and the rictal smile. Oh, his manners were urbane; you could tell that he'd traveled places and eaten in hotels and knew where the hoot owls hooted, but this was still a jumping-off place for him just the same. After all, what's a nickel-and-dime town out on a marsh to a god of death?

While unkind persons have suggested that the Baron couldn't tell the difference between his people and the living in Oysterback in the winter, we were all a little apprehensive about his visit. We don't get too many deities around here. About the best we usually do is the occasional self-proclaimed saintly woman who puts up with a rotten husband and ungrateful children. Death is certainly no stranger to us; we're about as mortal as the next town over, and maybe even more so, but still, to see the Baron moving among us, browsing the LaVyrle Spencer paperbacks at Omar Hinton's store, or enjoying a plate of goodies at the Ham and Oyster Supper down to the Fire Hall, or playing sixteen cards at once over at St. Morpheme's was something none of us ever quite got used to. It was like turning a corner and seeing someone mirrored in a plate glass window who doesn't look quite right, only to realize that you were looking at your own reflection.

You were somehow always sure that Baron Samedi was going to come after you in his professional role, even though he was on vacation, and as much as some people like to think that they are somehow prepared for death, few really are.

Still and all, he did love his Bingo, and Miss Florence, Miss Nettie, Miss Sister, and all of them certainly did enjoy having him to squire them out to the Golden Corral for dinner, then over to Tuesday Night Bingo at St. Morpheme's in Patamoke. Of course, Father Rothschild got a little red in the face when he met the Baron; Reverend Briscoe had had the same reaction, but they both got over it eventually. The Baron was not without his charm.

Still and all, when Junie drove Miss Florence and the Baron to BWI to catch their flight to Tallahassee last week, the whole marsh heaved a collective sigh of relief. Deities are fun to read about in *People*, but having them come to visit can be something of a strain.

"He's a nice enough fella," Junie confided to people afterward, "but a little stiff."

☺YSTERBACK  BUGEYE

Helga Wallop, Editor   PO Box 3, Oysterback MD 21000   25 cents

🦀 *Published every now and then or whenever there's news...* 🦀

Judge's Decoy Collection Among Finest in U.S. Says Jamboree Committee President

By Hon. Myrtle P. Goodyear
Mayor of Watertown
President,
Decoy Jamboree Weekend Committee
(Special to *The Bugeye*)

WATERTOWN-As excitement over the annual Decoy Jamboree Weekend continues to mount, a prominent Eastern Shore judge, decoy collector, and socialite prepares to judge an entirely different event that annually creates lots of excitement among downtown merchants and waterfowl decoy lovers everywhere who come to Watertown just for this annual excitement.

The Decoy Jamboree Weekend Special Supplement caught up with Judge Findley F. Fish at his palatial and tasteful waterfront gracious home in order to interview him about his part in Decoy Jamboree Weekend this coming month in Watertown. We were very excited about his affiliation with this exciting and prestigious event that is held once a year in Watertown.

Even though the Honorable Fish lives near Bethel in Devanau County, and not Watertown in Santimoke County, he has graciously agreed to serve once again on the Jamboree Committee which has many prominent Socialite Eastern Shore decoy collectors on it, including him.

He has the most prominent collection of all the collectors and is looked up to as a collector's collector of decoy waterfowl birds. Judge Fish is a metropolitist of the first rank who has been places and eaten in hotels and really knows his waterfowl bird decoys, which he has been collecting since a small boy.

His Honor Judge Fish says he has more than 1000 prominent decoys carved by famous decoy carvers in his house, and he has a whole room full of carved waterfowl birds around his swimming pool numbering more than 5000 more which is closed in all year around with glass shelves full of birds on the walls and is very unusual. He very graciously hosted a tour of the house which is palatially decorated in the Martha Stewart style by his wife Caroline who laying down with a headache and couldn't be interviewed for this article because and his collection in the pool room except for the ones in the study and the living room.

Judge says that he has many famous carvers like the Ward Brothers who were in the Washington Smithsonian Museum where their decoys cost six-figures, he says. Other decoys include Ira Hudson, Currier and Ives, Shang Wheeler, Umbrella Watson, Cigar Daisy, and many other Chesapeake Bay famous old makers and elsewhere.

(See Decoy p. 2)

(From Decoy p. 1)

His Honor Judge says it is the great ambition of his collection to own a Scratch Wallace as Scratch Wallace decoys are very, very rare and almost no one has them except some Japanese collectors who really prefer decorative bird carving because of their multiculturalism but a Scratch Wallace is so valuable that they will collect that because it is so valuable.

Scratch Wallace decoys are very old, rare, and valuable, he lived around Oysterback in the civil war but he died so he doesn't carve any more decoys. This makes them rare and valuable, especially if you are a Japanese cartel and want to spend a million dollars for a pair of canvasback ducks sleeping.

The decoys are also prized as antiques and Folk Art which is why many people collect them, but old-time hunters like he is really like to collect them because they used to hunt over the decoys when he was a boy. Mr. Fish thinks the carved and painted ducks and geese are very beautiful and says a true collector will do almost anything to own one of the really rare ones like a Scratch Wallace, which is very old and rare.

Although we wanted to talk and see all about Mr. Judge's individual collection, he didn't want to take pictures for the Godless communist media because of the insurance and the thieves who see them and steal decoys and sell them to other people who aren't so honest as collectors will do almost anything to collect those rare and exotic decoys.

Therefore, he has become quite seclusive about this because he doesn't want common sorry watermen and people breaking in and stealing his birds and some of them are rare, although he says it's not the trashy people he worries about but the other collectors, some of them quite prominently established socialite types of people whose names anyone would know at once will do anything to own a fine working waterfowl bird decoy like some of the ones in his collection even though they are quite famous and will even try to pass off a reproduction as the real thing, which he would never think of doing if the other person knew his birds. His judgeship says he is 100% honest collector who loves his decoys so much he will do anything himself to own one, even go and buy them.

Over Coffee and Mint Milanos in the decoy duck decorated kitchen the Judgefullness said he will do his best to judge all the working decoys just like he does court criminals with impartiality and fairness except when he knows they did it or are Godless communist and get sentenced to three years on jail carvers he doesn't like in court when they steal from his collection.

FERRUS T. BUCKETT'S STARLING SOLUTION

$\mathcal{S}$tarting around Groundhog Day, Ferrus T. Buckett begins to build his eel pots. Ferrus, as we all know, is the world's oldest waterman, being somewhere between seventy and death. But he still likes to put his pots overboard in March, when those eels begin to return to Chesapeake Bay from the Sargasso Sea.

Ferrus sets up his wire mesh and his clamps by the kerosene furnace in the kitchen where it's warm, and works away through the cold weather. For entertainment, he keeps a couple of bird feeders and a suet bag where he can see them out the window.

Ferrus is very attached to the titmice and the juncoes and the chickadees that come to his porch. He attracts all kinds of birds to his feeders, Ferrus does. He's got a mockingbird and a couple of flickers that come around regularly, and climb all over the suet bag he's hung from the cedar tree. He's partial to the redwings that hop all over the porch rails, too. The little sparrows are so tame that they cluster around the feeder when they see him coming with an old coffee can full of seed, and it amuses him no end to look out the windows at the squabbling jays and the bright cardinals. He'll work and watch the nuthatches climbing down the trees head first; their antics make him laugh, the way they flutter back and forth and chitter at each other. At dawn, when he's making coffee, he watches the doves pick around the grass for cracked corn. Ferrus is a man who loves his birds. Why, he ran his workboat through a rig of seaduck decoys last winter because he loathes people who kill birds they can't even eat, just for fun.

But Francis of Assisi, Ferrus is not, as we found out when he had an invasion of English starlings a couple of weeks ago. Starlings, as some of you might know, are the bully boys of the bird world. Big, ugly-tempered, speckled creatures, they have the charm and personality of the current Congress, to whom they bear more than a passing resemblance. Not only do they drive all the other birds away, they fight with each other, poop all over, and generally hog up every food item in sight. They can clean out a good-sized feeder in about fifteen minutes flat, then hang around the door eyeing you as if you were a big sunflower seed-studded suet ball, daring you to come outside and fight, you pacifist *poulet* you. (As some will recall, Ferrus speaks perfect, Parisian French.)

Ferrus's general philosophy is *chacun à son goût*, and he realizes if you feed one bird, you feed them all, but starlings are something else entirely. He'd like to feed those starlings his dog Blackie's yellow snow. After this mob had hung around for several days, jabbering, dropping their doo everywhere, fighting and freeloading, driving all the other birds away, Ferrus finally decided he'd had enough; the starlings had to go. Ferrus thought as he worked on his pots and as he worked, he found the perfect solution. (You don't get to be the world's oldest waterman by being stupid.)

That afternoon, Ferrus went out on the marsh where the Boone Bros. keep their still and borrowed a compound bucket of sour mash off Gabe and Mike. He may have bought a jar of their five-hundred proof for himself while he was there, but we can't say that for sure. We do know that he came back and spread that mash all around his porch where even the dullest of the dull-witted starlings wouldn't miss it. Then he picked up his wire and his clamps and went back to building eel pots, humming contentedly to himself, like he does when he's up to something.

Those greedy starlings couldn't get enough of that mash. By lunchtime, they were staggering around and slurring their words. Drunk? Who them? Why they could pry flerfectly well, yank thoo! But just annuder one for the road, ya know? Ferrus listened to them

befuddledly slamming into the screen door as they tried to take off and chuckled when a red tail hawk dive-bombed the porch and they all just rolled across the yard, too stoned to flee.

When he looked out again around suppertime, there were about one hundred of them passed out all over the concrete like so many speckled lumps from a moldy featherbed. Grabbing a bushel basket, he walked outside and loaded up the stuporous fowl. He called Blackie and loaded the snoring starling basket into the back of his pickup.

Ferrus caught up with Paisley Redmond just as he was about to set out from the seafood plant with a truckload of Cap'n Fike's Flash Frozen Breaded Clam Strips bound for Cambridge. Ferrus slipped his bushel basket load of inebriated starlings into the back of Paisley's truck and gave him precise directions to Phil Gramm's gunning estate down near Blackwater. Senator Gramm, who proclaimed his Eastern Shore neighbors stupid, was, to Ferrus's mind, the perfect host for a flock of European starlings.

By the time those birds woke up, they'd have fierce hangovers and worse attitudes than even Phil himself. And they'd be too disoriented to ever find their way back to Ferrus's house again.

It was, to his mind, the perfect starling solution.

"You know, honey," Ferrus told Blackie as they headed home again, and he was feeling philosophical, "some fool wanted to introduce all the birds mentioned in Shakespeare to the New World. So he let a pack of European starlings loose in Central Park, in New York. He's dead now, but they've just kept on goin', gettin' out of hand."

Blackie snuffled and cocked his head.

"But," Ferrus continued thoughtfully, "I'd like to bring that man back to life. Just so I could kill him all over again. And you know how?"

Blackie yawned.

"I'd have him pecked to death by starlings," Ferrus chuckled, as he wheeled into Omar Hinton's parking lot to pick up a thirty-pound bag of birdseed.

OYSTERBACK BUGEYE

Helga Wallop, Editor   PO Box 3, Oysterback MD 21000   25 cents

❧ Published every now and then or whenever there's news... ❧

What's What in Wallopsville
Social Notes by Mrs. Louisa "Sister" Gibbs

The lemonade flowed and a good time was had by all when View 'n' Chew owners Delmar P. and Earlene Tuttle celebrated the Alley Gators' Tuesday Night Bowling League Tourney victory with a Fish Fry for team members, family, friends, and customers in the parking lot of the store. Earlene barbecued up plenty of hardheads in her secret sauce for all and sundry, while music was provided by Delmar P., whose rendition of the "Jesus Loves Me Polka" was a toe-tapping success. Some may remember that Delmar P. placed second after Nils Lofgren in the 1971 Maryland State Accordion Championships.

Purvis and Susie Lou Toadvine and family are visiting Captain and Mrs. Lennie Skinner at their rental cottage in Ocean City this week. . .

Winkie Bugg and Whack Wallace are visiting Whack's niece Tahnee Rae and her family near Atlantic City this week. Winkie and Whack hope to get some blackjack in at the casinos, as they are anxious to test their new system, which Whack received in a dream from Senator Paul Sarbanes while sleeping on the couch at Winkie's during the big ice storm last winter when the power was down at her house. Good luck, girls!

Methodist Women reports that the Cantaloupe Festival took in more than $500 toward the purchase of a new air-conditioning system for the church.

The old one was ruined, readers will recall, when a family of skunks took up their abode there last spring and church sexton Purnell Pruitt ran into the unit with the Lawn Boy when mowing and not paying attention. Iva says Purnell is almost ready to stop living in the boat house and come indoors again. She reports you can hardly smell him anymore at all...

Betty Price, over to Santimoke Community Cable TV, announces that the system will be adding The O.J. Simpson Channel to their lineup this week. "All O.J., All the Time" should satisfy the cravings of many morbid curiosity seekers now that they've put a traffic light in on "Dead Man's Intersection" at County Road 393 and Route 50. . .

Chickie Farmer is wondering why Litey Clash has to import professionals from Baltimore to enter his wet t-shirt contests at Liteyworld, his new Ocean City bar, when so many talented locals are unemployed. . .

Mrs. Asahael Gloom Phipps and Mrs. Button Hicks of the Josiah Whaley Chapter of the Daughters of Famous Tories were hostesses of the monthly chapter meeting, held at Mount Boredom, the historical old mansion. Guest lecturer was E. Power Tutweiler, who spoke to the Daughters on the importance of historical ancestors,

(See Notes p. 2)

(From Notes p. 1)

especially now that the Godless Liberal Media are having them too. Historically accurate refreshments included Martha Jefferson's bridge mix and Queen Victoria's Pigs-in-a-Blanket.

Former Jodie's Fashion Whirl Boutique employees Imogene Pickering and Sudie Fairbank met some people in a VW Van on Route 301 and are now spending the summer following Phish on their current concert tour with them. Gregg says Imogene's latest postcard came from Portland. She says to forward her Social Security check and that Sudie is getting her navel pierced, if she can find it.

That was Barlow Wiggins on *Springer* last week. For those of you who missed the episode, the theme was "Cross Dressing Soybean Farmers Who Believe They are in Contact with Uranus."

The Wallopsville Volunteer Hook and Ladder Company won the Best Float contest at the Old West Hundred Days parade over to Patamoke last week. Chief Gloria Hinton reports their float theme was "Famous Wallopsville Poultry Products."

Venus Tutweiler hostessed the monthly meeting of Great Books at her home in the Shallow Shores Doublewide Park last Tuesday. Guests included Venus's sister Lavonda Hardcastle, June Grubb, Rochelle Fosbreath, and Fern Legume. The works of Italo Calvino were discussed, and Heloise Helk, who on vacation with her husband Waldo in West Virginia, was nominated Refreshment Committee Chairwoman for the coming year.

Popular local song stylist Raeline Boudine is visiting her cousin Francine Boudine in Port Deposit this week. Raeline will be singing new songs of her own composition at the Peach Bottom Moonlite Bay Supper Club, accompanied by Francine on cocktail organ and sister Martine on drums. Raeline plans to wear a chartreuse satin gown of her own design with sequins, seed pearls, and shoes dyed to match. Her brother, Racine Boudine of Essex, will be recording her songs for Talent Night at the Patamoke Theater in the Oblong where she was a semi-finalist last year and won many fine prizes including a free car wash at Ray Bob's Gas 'n' Go and a complimentary manicure at Doreen's Curl Up 'n' Dye Salon de Beaute over to Oysterback featuring Revlon's Rusty Rose Nail Enamel.

Billy and Lisa Chinaberry and baby Clint are visting Captain and Mrs. Lennie Skinner at their rental cottage in Ocean City next week.

OCCURENCE AT OYSTERBACK BRIDGE:
AN ORAL HISTORY OF AN ODD EVENT

MISS NETTIE LEERY: I got up one morning and looked out my kitchen window and there it was, big as life. Bigger; the thing must have been about ten by twelve, just stuck down there on a stob right there on Oysterback Creek, by the bridge, so you could see it as you were coming into town. A great big old sign that said "LITEY CLASH'S DEW DROP INN AND LITEY-WORLD BAR THURSDAY IS ALWAYS WET T-SHIRT NIGHT." All in huge purple and gold lettering with that sequin-y stuff on it, like you see on those billboards outside of Ocean City, you know, very tacky. And below that, there was just little tiny lettering with his oyster bed lease number on it. Honey, that thing was ug-lee, I'm here to tell you! It just ruined my beautiful view of the water. It was like someone'd stuck a plastic flower in a field of roses...his mother was a Glack, you know. *Most* of the Clashes are very nice people.

DESIREE GRINCH: Well, you just have to know Litey Clash, that's all. He craves attention the way some people crave chocolate. Never mind if it's negative, it's still attention. I, Desiree Grinch, proprietor of the Blue Crab Tavern (★★★ *Guide Michelin*) am a businesswoman, and I understand the value of publicity. But if Litey'd paid as much attention to the quality of his food and drink as he did to that prank, he wouldn't need a sign like that, would he? People'd be over to the Dew

Drop in busloads, wouldn't they? He only did it to get attention. And succeeded.

HUDSON SWANN: The packing houses have been leasing oyster bottom from the state around here for years. What you do is, you sink a stob and nail up a piece of board with your number on it, so everyone knows it's your leased bed, and they're supposed to keep off. Supposed to, anyway. Some don't, but that's another story.

JUNIOR REDMOND: But what Litey done was, he leased that bed and stuck up a great big old sign on there advertising his bar. Which was, you gotta admit, a clever idea. Of course, people in the West Hundred complained, but what does Litey care?

DOREEN REDMOND: He doesn't live out there, and his cousin Juanita's on the zoning board, if you know what I mean and I think you do. Come to find out there was no law against it! But no one ever did it before either. Well!

HUDSON SWANN: And so it just sat there, ugly as sin. Folks out here were up in arms, and some heated letters flew back and forth in the *Bugeye*.

HELGA WALLOP: Well, Litey called me, and I went out to cover it, because I figured it was a story. The *Bugeye* is a newspaper. But after I wrote it up, I thought to myself why should I give him free advertising? I thought just let 'em all slug it out in letters to the editor, and if the county or the DNR or the Coast Guard gets into it, I'll print that. Listen, I may be an editor, but I have to live in this town. But we did get some letters.

DOREEN REDMOND: Most people were appalled. It was an intrusion. It set an ugly precedent, sitting there where you had to see it when you went over the bridge to Oysterback. Pretty soon, you could just see that anyone with a business would lease some bottom and jam up a big old sign for their business all over the water.

DESIREE GRINCH: Oh, mud was flung and names were called! I've never seen anything that united this community like that sign. They were all against it. Except for one...

PARSONS DREEDLE: Well, I thought it was kind of clever. Said so in my letter to the paper. Wish I'd thought of it myself. Be a good place to advertise my funeral home and produce stand, on a sign like that. Sort of improve on nature a little, I thought. That's what I told the TV cameras, too.

DOREEN REDMOND: This from a man with a yard full of Virgin Marys in birdbaths, pink flamingoes, bendovers, and duck whirligigs!

LYMOND V. "SNAKE" WINGATE: Litey says to me, he says, whyn't you write a letter to the *Bugeye* over the sign? So I did. I writes, "I don't see why you're all fussing about a handsome, trim sign like that over that nasty old rotten bridge over that dirty ole creek."

DESIREE GRINCH: I heard Litey gave him a case a beer to write that letter. Snake always did work cheap!

JUNIOR REDMOND: Well, it weren't too long before someone mysteriously came along and sawed that sign right on off the stob. Happened in the dead of night, we think.

HELGA WALLOP: Litey wanted that story in the paper, too. I ran it. Why not? It was a news story. He fussed and fumed and said the Oysterback watermen were out to get him. Offered a great big reward for whoever did it. That's news. Litey was getting his name up everywhere, without having to shell out a cent.

HUDSON SWANN: Well, I knew I didn't do it!

JUNIOR REDMOND: Me, neither. First ice come up there, it would heave it right over, so why bother? Till he come around us, I thought the whole thing was pretty funny...until my name got dragged into it.

DESIREE GRINCH: He came up here and ranted and raved and pointed the finger and all but wanted us all arrested. I don't have time to go out there and chainsaw a sign down. Unlike some of us, I have a very busy business to run. But he was determined to pin it on somebody, so of course it had to be Junie and Huddie.

HELGA WALLOP: You have to admit, those two boys are likely to be around when there's mischief!

JUNIOR REDMOND: So, when Sheriff Briscoe come around with a warrant, and they found that Liteyworld sign behind my shed, it looked bad. Real bad. I never saw it before! Ask Doreen!

HUDSON SWANN: Me neither. But I tell you this, neither of us never sawed down that sign. Litey was talking about pressing charges though. Now, that was all over the news. A nine day's wonder.

HELGA WALLOP: Well, it *was* news. And I'm in business to report the news. So's the TV and the radio, and they all had the story, too. But I never said Huddie and Junie did it. I have to live in this town.

DESIREE GRINCH: Don't you know, he called a press conference when he put that sign back up, bigger and better than before, with a big old spotlight trained right on it, so you could see it all over the marsh at night.

HELGA WALLOP: And he said, he said, something to the effect that he knew that there would be "further assults on an honest businessman" that the "show wasn't over yet." It's in my notebook.

DESIREE GRINCH: That's what made me stop and think.

CHIEF BRISCOE: Which was how Johnny Ray and I ended up in the cruiser behind the bridge for a couple of long, cold nights.

DEPUTY JOHNNY RAY INSLEY: It didn't take too long. The third night, we saw that big old Lincoln Town Car come rumbling over the bridge and we knew we had the truth.

CHIEF BRISCOE: Johnny Ray had an idea and borrowed Miss Nettie's video camera, got it all on tape. There was ole Litey Clash, big as life, with Snake Wingate right beside him, takin' a chain saw to his own sign!

DEPUTY JOHNNY RAY: We had him dead to rights. Snake confessed he'd planted that sign behind Junie's shed. Revenge for last year's softball playoffs, he said.

DESIREE GRINCH: You have to hand it to Litey, he knows how to attract attention. He just has to have some attention, doesn't care what kind. It's very sad. But it backfired on him. I hear tell that people were so offended by the sign that they began to stay away from the Dew Drop Inn in droves.

DOREEN REDMOND: Still, when people tell me they want to get themselves a lukewarm beer and a crabcake the size of a baby's fist floating in a hogshead of grease, I nearly always tell them to head down to Wingo to the Dew Drop Inn.

THE MEANEST MAN IN
DEVANAU COUNTY

*T*hank you, thank you very much, Operator. Operator? Hello, is that you, Miss Desiree? Thanks for accepting the collect call. What? Oh, yeah, it's me, Wade, and Mookie. Say hello to Miss Desiree, Mookie! Hear him! Aw, Miss Desiree, be nice. What? You'll have to speak up, it's pretty noisy in here. Jail? Na, we're not in jail, heh, heh, heh. Na, we're up to Baltimore. What? Oh. Mookie wanted to see Tawnee, so we come up to Port Deposit last night, but she was out, so we come on over to Baltimore. Yeah, we're over to the Cameo Lounge on Harford Road. What? Now why would Miss Marge throw us out? Well, yeah, there is that, but we're behavin' ourselves, honest. Yeah. I'll tell her. Yes, ma'm, I will tell her what you said.

No, Mookie's right here next to me by the pay phone. I can see what he's doin' all the time. What? Oh, yeah. No I can't put Miss Marge on the phone, she's upstairs. Yeah, I guess she doesn't know we're here or she *would* throw us out. Hey, Nick, can we have a couple more of them beers over here? Thanks. Pay the man, Mookie.

What? You've gotta speak up; I can't hear too good over Mookie. What? Oh, yeah. Naw, it's not an emergency or nothin', we just had this great idea. Yes ma'm, the Wade Man and the Mookster have been thinkin'. What? You could smell something burnin'? Aw, Miss Desiree, is that any way to talk? I mean, here we is, and we got this great idea and we want to cut you in on it. We need you to rent the ring. The ring. No, no, the boxing ring. So we're calling you—the boxing ring for the elimination boxing match we're gonna set up!

No, no, listen! Listen! This ain't like that, this is for real, a good idea and we can all make a fortune off of it. We can do it at your bar, in the parking lot. What? The Meanest Man in Devanau County Contest. Yes, you can finally go to the Caribbean and drink Mai Tais with Harrison Ford when we—what? Well, of course! No, this isn't like the time we let alla them chickens outta that truck. Besides, that wasn't our fault, them chickens just followed us home, that's all. We're gonna have a contest! To see who the meanest man in the county is! Hell, I know Haney Sparks is dead! But there's plenty more of them around—What? What kind of contest? No, of course not. Mookie ain't *that* drunk. No, Miss Desiree, you gotta listen, because the Mooker and I think this is a good idea and we could all make a lotta money on this, if it's done right. Why do we need you? What? Turn that damn thing down, Mookie, I can barely hear Miss Desiree!

Hello? Hello, you there? Good. You don't want to lose out on this one, Miss Desiree, we all gonna make us some money on this. It's the The Meanest Man in Devanau County Contest. What? No, not the *greenest* man, the *meanest* man. Dammit, Mookie, will you give Nick a couple bucks for them beers or do I have to slap you upside your dumb head? Not you, Miss Desiree. I was talkin' to Mookie. It's an elimination boxing match. What? No, our idea! Well, we seen this movie on cable and—Mookie, stop that! Leave that girl alone!

Yes, I'm back. Now, look, Miss Desiree, here's our idea. What? Our idea! Mookie, let that girl alone, she's got a great big ole boyfriend sittin' right over there, you fool. Miss Desiree, you there? Hello? Hello? Yeah, listen, Miss Desiree, we wanna run a contest. Yeah, a contest! No, we ain't gonna try and sell your bar by lottery, that didn't work the last time we tried it. No, I swear, Miss Desiree, this is gonna work. No, really. See, what we're gonna do is hold an elimination boxing match to see who the meanest man in Devanau County really is. What? What? Aw, Miss Desiree, lissen, this one is a good idea, we can't hardly lose on this one. Mookie, will you cut that out? Na, what we wanna do is charge alla them guys who think they're so tough twenty bucks to get in the ring and pound each other into sand, and the winner gets the purse. What? What?

Dammit, Mookie, *will* you stop that? Hey! Hey you, yeah, you! I'm talking to you! Let him alone, ma'm, he's a fool and don't know no better than to try to mess with someone else's girlfriend. Tell the lady you're sorry, Mookie. He don't mean nothing wrong, ma'am. He's just as dumb as a chunk, that's all. Mookie, will you stop that, right now? Hello, Miss Desiree, you still there? I gotta talk fast, Miss Marge just come in and told us to leave. Yes, I will tell her you said hello. What?

Yeah, Miss Desiree, that's our idea. What else? Whattya mean what else? Well, we *did* want to hold it in your parking lot, and we thought you could put up the money for advertising, and the tickets and the concessions and the rental of the ring, and we could split the proceeds right down the middle, but—hello? Hello? Damn, Mookie, will you cut that out? Miss Desiree? You there, Miss Desiree? Hello? Hello? Miss Desiree? You there? Hello?

Wow, Mookie, I think she hung up on me.

She did hang up on me.

Now, why do you suppose would she want to do something like that?

AN OYSTERBACK LETTER TO SANTA

Dear Santa,

I know it has been a while since you have heard from me, Desiree Grinch, proprietor of the Blue Crab Tavern over to Oysterback, but times being what they are, I didn't think you would mind if I dropped you a line.

When I was little, I used to get you and God mixed up. You know, long white beards, old white European males, etc., but I think I have it right now. Anyway, some of the stuff on my Christmas list may take a miracle.

This year, please make sure that Captain Hardee Swann's Christmas lights are the best in the neighborhood. Last year, he heard there was Mr. Travers over to Cambridge with a new twenty-foot creche scene and 70,000 more lights, so he just *had* to plug in that forty-year-old string of bubble lights he found at a yard sale. Added to the forty-three illuminated figures and the 69,900 lights he already had up, it overloaded the transformer something terrible. The sparks were beautiful, but no one around here liked being without power for two days. It was nice of the power company to give him his own transformer this year.

Doreen wants thirty minutes alone in the bathroom, without one of the kids or the dogs or Junie coming in, asking dumb questions about where they put stuff that's right under their noses, for pete's sake. She would also like five minutes with Fabio, but let's get real here.

Also, could you see your way clear to getting Huddie at least a B on his English final at the community college? Going back to school at forty is tough.

Junie would like the oysters to hold out till the end of the month, so he doesn't have to start house painting for rich people until the new year and mess up his taxes.

Omar Hinton could use a poke in the eye with a sharp stick after the way he voted on that sewer bill last council meeting, but I hope you will bring him a new satellite dish to replace the one Alonzo Deaver broke when he fell off that DNR helicopter he stole jacklighting deer that time last fall.

Although he probably deserves ashes and coal, Alonzo could probably use some commissary privileges over to the Detention Center.

You don't have to bring Sudie Fairbank anything; she won the lottery for $2.8 million and bought herself a new doublewide.

You ought to be bringing Miss Nettie Leery a trip to visit her sister in San Diego; cold weather is awful hard on her arthritis, and she could finally get to go see *Wheel of Fortune*, her favorite show, being taped.

I personally think you should motivate Parsons Dreedle to get up the nerve to pop the question to Ella Sparks. He's been sweet on her since high school, and she's been a widow for more than a year now. He opens and closes his mouth and the words just won't come out for him, he's been an old funeral director bachelor so long. If he doesn't propose to her soon, I am going to offer her a job cooking for the Blue Crab. Talent like that is too good to pass up. Besides, I think every story deserves a happy ending.

I hope you will forgive Ferrus for saying he doesn't believe in Christmas. And besides, we both know who was Santa's Helper over to the Head Start Christmas party last Saturday. Bah, humbug, huh? Ferrus could sure use a new set of foul weather gear, but I think what he really wants is some new Edith Piaf tapes. I have a feeling World War II must have been very interesting for Ferrus.

Helga says she hopes Poot isn't planning to try to pass off the new dryer as her Christmas present. Knowing how cheap Poot is, I wouldn't be surprised. That man is as tight as a tick and brags about it. Maybe you should bring Fabio to Helga; she could use the change.

Whatever Fabio is, I'll bet even money he's not cheap.

When Hagar Jump asked me what I wanted the other day down to the Post Office, I said an eighteen-year-old boyfriend and a million dollars in the bank. I was just kidding of course, or maybe not, but it does make you think. That reminds me, Earl Don needs one of those beaded seat things for the power company truck, if he has to drive it all day long.

Personally, I would be satisfied with an airtight alibi and a foolproof plan, if you get around to it.

Your Friend,

Desiree
Proprietor, Blue Crab Tavern

P.S. World peace and a clean planet would be nice.

THE LAST WORD IN CHRISTMAS LIGHTS

Dear Santa,

Thanks for your nice response to my last letter. I, Desiree Grinch, proprietor of the Blue Crab Tavern, would like to take this opportunity to let you know how much we all appreciated your visit last year, and to apologize again for the misunderstanding. Alonzo Deaver has sworn off drinking Pride of Baltimore Vodka when he's jacklighting deer, so Rudolph should have no unpleasantness this year. Again, we are all very sorry about that.

Also, I'm sorry you had so much trouble finding us way out on the marsh, but to tell you the truth, sometimes we have some trouble finding ourselves, if you know what I mean, and I think you do.

Anyway, I didn't think you would mind if I dropped you a line again this year and sort of brought you up to speed on what's been happening down here.

As always, there's always this little matter of Captain Hardee Swann's Christmas lights. There's this Captain Plunk Pickett over to Wingo, Virginia, with a whole big bunch of moving Christmas figures and holiday display cases and pre-recorded caroling music and elves, sleighs, snowmen, and Santas and maybe five or six more lights than Mr. Hardee has, which makes Mr. Hardee crazy, since it is his ambition to be the King of Christmas Lights, and he and this Mr. Plunk have a life-long rivalry left over from their days as skipjack captains, the origins of which are lost in the mists of time, as Professor Shepherd says. It may be lost in the mists of time, but those two sure haven't lost track of it, and Christmas is the time when they bring it all out and paste it up all over their houses for the world to see, then plug it all in. God forbid one of them should have one less Tiny Twinkle Light than the other.

Last year, Mr. Hardee got some of those three-dimensional wire figures from the flea market over to Seaford. Added to the 69,999 lights he picked up at Earlene and Delmar P.'s yard sale, it looked real good and gave off a nice, post-nuclear glow you could see all the way to Tubman's Corners. But then he heard a rumor that Mr. Plunk had gone to the black market and purchased the legendary Computo Lite 5000 Bulb Serial Set that alternately flashes out MERRY CHRISTMAS and HAPPY NEW YEAR in traveling blinkers.

Normally, you have to be a pro to possess these lights. You have to be a registered retail display operator or a licensed dealer to own these mega-watt, computerized babies. In some states, there's talk of registering Computo Lite 5000 Bulb Serial Sets, to keep them out of the hands of amateurs, but Mr. Hardee and Mr. Plunk agreed that if Computo Lites are outlawed, only outlaws will have them.

Still, I guess Mr. Hardee thought his chestnuts were fried when he got word about that.

But then, at South of the Border on her way back from Florida last April, Florence Redmond picked up a 1986 Elko 43-Piece Illuminated Nativity Set and Mr. Hardee knew there was a Supreme Being who smiled on him.

The Elko '86 43-Piece Illuminated Nativity Set is the jewel in the crown of any serious Christmas light enthusiast, including as it does the Grazing Donkey discontinued in later sets because of complaints that it fell over in high winds. Of course, you do have the '86 edition Melchior who looks like Lyle Alzado, but that's a small price to pay for the glory of knowing you own a collector's dream. Compared to an '86 Elko Nativity, Computo Lites are birthday candles.

Well, you know what happened. It happens every year. At first dark the day after Thanksgiving, Mr. Hardee overloaded the transformer the power company gave him, and blew his Life Size Good Shepherd of Graceland Reverently Illuminated Elvis Figure all the way out to the Bay, where it landed on a Japanese freighter and gave some innocent Nissan Stanzas a whole new look. The sailors in the Shipping Channel said they thought Calvert Cliffs had finally gone off, or so we heard later.

After he got his wiring straightened out and Oysterback was bathed in a warm mid-day radiance, Mr. Hardee, gloating with anticipated triumph, hopped in the truck and drove down to Wingo.

When he got to Mr. Plunk's house, he was astonished to find it was decorated with only a tasteful Christmas wreath. Not a lite in site, so to speak. Mrs. Plunk, a woman of the sinisterly tasteful Martha Stewart school, sadly informed Mr. Hardee that Mr. Plunk had passed over last August, his truly astonishing Christmas Lights Collection dispersed among his children and grandchildren.

But the late Plunk, she told Mr. Hardee, was determined to have the last word. If Mr. Hardee would drive past the Wingo Memorial Garden of Rest, he would see that his old rival had left a posthumous message.

Privately thinking this was Christmas, not Halloween, Mr. Hardee expressed his deepest sympathies to the widow and took himself off past the boneyard. He had no trouble locating the late Plunk's tombstone.

Powered by an old marine battery, that Computo Lite 5000 Bulb Serial Set that alternately flashed out MERRY CHRISTMAS and HAPPY NEW YEAR in traveling blinkers was tastefully draped around Mr. Plunk's tombstone.

Talk about having the last word.

Your Friend,

Desiree
Proprietor, Blue Crab Tavern

P.S. Any leads on that eighteen-year-old and million bucks?

AN AGE OF ICE AND MAGIC

*W*hen winter came, it had teeth. For a week, the wind came in from the northeast, just as sharp and cold as a Republican's heart. Ice storm after ice storm downed power lines and cut off the phones, coating the world with a thin, frigid beauty, slicing the village of Oysterback off from the outside world. At night, in the cold black stillness, the crack of trees breaking beneath the weight of the ice sounded like rifle shots in the darkness. The boats were cradled up in the ice at the harbor; little traffic moved on the slick roads. The sky itself stayed gray and sullen. After a few days, the ice grew so dense that folks actually walked out into the middle of the shipping channel. For one brief moment there was awe, as they understood they were *standing* in the middle of the Chesapeake Bay, and there was ice as far as the eye could see. Time itself was frozen in the ice, suspended between then and now.

Hudson Swann only walked out onto the narrow channel between Uranusville Marsh and the eroding stand of pines that used to be Swann's Island. Fifty, seventy-five years ago, there were houses, even a store and post office there, and that's where his people lived, but wind and water have worn it all away until it's little more than a cripple in the estuary where the Devanau flows into the Chesapeake. Even the old graves are disappearing into the Bay, the thin gray stones like teeth in the ice along the banks of the island.

What Hudson's got in mind may be legal, or it may not be legal, but he's carrying his chainsaw and what he means to do with it is open up a hole big enough to stick a pair of nippers down into an oyster bed about five feet below the surface. He just wants a half bushel or so for supper, enough to feed his family. Hudson Swann is not a greedy man, just a hungry one, and as he starts the chainsaw, the sound of it echoes off the pines, shaking ice and needles down on the gravestones.

He braces himself on the ice and begins to cut at the surface like a sculptor, intent on slicing it away just so; chips fly in all directions before he thinks he sees what looks like a fish staring back up at him, except it's more like a person than a fish, then more like a fish than a person. Whatever it is, the sight of it stops him, and he bends over to look at it closely. It's trapped in the ice, whatever it is, and it has large, fishy, pleading eyes that are looking right up at him.

Gently, like a marble sculptor, Hudson begins to work around it, and when he's done all he can with the chainsaw, he unfolds his Buck knife and kneels on the hard ice, chipping away patiently until a face is visible in the ice. It's not a face like any other face he's ever seen, and it's more than ever somewhere between a fish and a person, the muddy green color of the Devanau, and the black eyes are blinking now as the cold air begins to hit the green, iridescent scales. Then the mouth, like the mouth of a rockfish, opens and closes. It's making low, nervous noises, like moans crying as it defrosts, a cold blooded creature.

Hudson supposes he should be frightened, but he feels as if he doesn't have time for that because he's busy trying to chip the ice away from its gills, and now it's trying to help him, its delicately veined, webbed hands struggling to push itself up and down through the ice, working its way out of its cold prison. At last, with a great breaking roar of ice, it's freed, rising from the black water and spreading its green, finned arms in a wide, joyful arc, its long fishy tail flaying the air in pure celebration. And Hudson Swann, ducking flying ice and water, sees, as she sinks back into the hole, that he has freed a mermaid from the ice.

For just a moment, she floats in the black water, her long green hair spreading out around her, looking up at Hudson from her world beneath the water, and Hudson looks back at her from his world above the water, and then she's gone, with just a silver flash of that long fish-tail and a look before she disappears beneath the surface, black water closing around her.

For a long time, Hudson stands gazing out into the iceblink, feeling her path with his heart as she swims beneath the ice, out of the Devanau River and into the currents of the Chesapeake, heading out to sea, and for just one moment, frozen in time, he knows that he could follow her, swimming beneath the ice, drifting on the currents of the cold black water, swimming away from this tired old world toward another place where the sun always shines and the eldritch magic still works.

And then slowly, just a little older, he turns and walks carefully across the ice to get his nippers out of the truck.

He hums to himself as he walks, feeling his heavy old boots weighing him down against the surface of the earth.

IT'S THE END OF THE WORLD
AS WE KNOW IT

*A*round the time the shadbush blooms, Reverend Claude Crouch, The Traveling Evangelist, drives the Godmobile into Oysterback. The Godmobile is actually a '79 Sierra, but since Claude has covered the body and the cap in his unique version of spray painted Scripture, it's the Godmobile.

Things have not been going too well for Claude since the last time we saw him. He quit shifting gears for God at the True Doctrine Transmission Shop in Virginia Beach after some unpleasantness with the secular authorities, and those Condos for Christ over to Crisfield went up on flames, so to speak. And then some know-it-all critic panned his visionary chainsaw art sculptures in the *Sun*; said they lacked soul. ("As if some white, j-school suburban punk from Philadelphia would know *soul* if it bit him on the ass," Claude says.) He's getting old, he's getting tired, and what he would like to get himself is one of those cable TV preaching shows in a nice warm studio somewhere, but it's not likely that will happen anytime soon. So, Claude and all his worldly possessions, living all crammed up in the back of the Godmobile, remain on the sawdust trail.

"That comet's here! The end of the world is coming Saturday," Claude informed Omar Hinton when he stopped past the store to get a Diet Dr. Pepper and a slab of Macho Nacho. "I seen it. Angels will be in Uranusville Marsh on Saturday evening at sunset," he told all the old retired watermen and farmers who hang around in there.

Wasn't anybody laughing, either; Claude has no sense of humor, and some of us have seen some of his prophecies come true. Even Hudson Swann and Junior Redmond, who were in there buying extra bull lips, didn't laugh. It was Claude who diagnosed Junie's hepatica and laid on hands for it. And you know, Junie hasn't had any trouble with his hepatica since.

"World will end next Saturday dusk, when the angels come," Claude repeated. "The comet is here." He walked right on out of there and got back in his truck, drove down to Uranusville Marsh, parked in the state lot the hunters and trappers use, and set up his camp to wait for the attention he knew would come.

Word spread around the West Hundred the way a hawk's passing between the earth and the sun spreads out over the marsh. While there was no panic in the streets (that would require an outlay of energy and effort in the middle of gearing up for crabbing and tourists), there was some mild interest.

But we're a cynical lot.

"You wait and see. It'll be like that time he saw those aliens taking over the seafood plant and they turned out to be illegal workers from Iran, not Uranus," Doreen grumbled around a mouthful of bobby pins down at the Curl Up 'n' Dye Salon de Beaute. "But I'm still gonna get a gallon of milk and some extra toilet paper, just in case."

Which sort of summed up the way everyone thought about the upcoming event; nobody was canceling their dental appointments or putting off paying the bills, or at least not any more than usual.

Helga Wallop, who edits the *Bugeye*, our local paper, had to borrow Professor Shepherd's dictionary to see how to spell Armageddon.

She still spelled it wrong.

"If it's the end of the world and angels are coming, well, then, I want to see it, that's all, I just want to see it," Professor Shepherd told Desiree Grinch. As a Jeffersonian Deist, he was naturally skeptical, but still not taking any chances. Desiree, being Desiree, was more blunt about it; she didn't want to miss anything, not even the end of the world, and she intended to be there with bells on. "And I'm packin' a box supper, too," she added. "You never know."

As it turned out, a buzzard flock perched on the satellite dish over to Wallopsville and the West Hundred cable system went down on Saturday night about six. So even people who had planned an evening of *Cops* and *America's Most Wanted* suddenly found themselves at loose ends, and the West Hundred High School's baseball game with Wingo Consolidated got rained out, which left some more people with unexpected time on their hands. So, come sunset there was quite a ground gathered down on the state parking lot on Uranusville Marsh Road, waiting to see the end of the world.

The West Hundred likes a good revival as much as the next high place in the road, so you knew Claude would get a good turnout anyways. Why, some of us have been born again as much as three or four times, and Junior Redmond has repented so many times that he has frequent prayer miles. Besides, Claude always has a theme to his preaching, and when it's something good like the end of the world, almost everyone was a little interested to hear what he had to say. The Wallopsville Fire and Rescue brought along their Wiener Wagon and a Basket of Cheer Raffle; West Hundred Charge Methodist Women had a tailgate bake sale and Country Craft draw; and Desiree sold cold drinks out of the ice chest in the back of her monster truck, so people were satisfied to sit on top of their cars and watch the sun turn into a big red ball as it dropped toward the Western Shore. It was a wonderful sunset, the way a sunset is after a spring rain. It turned the whole marshland all shades of pink and purple and orange, and painted the sky.

Claude did himself up right; told us all we were sinners and bound for hell unless we changed our evil ways. Desiree Grinch muttered something about the company in hell being more interesting, but otherwise, most folks pretty much agreed with Claude's line of reasoning, which I will not bore you with, since most of you have heard Claude the first time. Suffice to say that many caught fire in the spirit that twilight on the marsh, and whether it was from God's gift of a heartbreakingly beautiful sunset over the water or Claude's exhortations, it is not my place to judge. The mood was on the mob, and the full moon was on the rise, no more than a silver coin in the darkening sky, and the stars and the comet—that wondrous comet with its wondrous tail hurtling through the universe—began to twinkle faintly in the gloom. Far away, there was the glitter of something else, too, somewhere between the sky and the horizon, but no one noticed that, or least not too much.

"Just as the sun's sinkin' down over that marsh, and darkness is creepin' across the land, so God is gonna end this here world of sin and material goods!" Claude shouted. "And there will come an angel who will announce the end of the world!" The sun was no more than a sliver in the water, and the silver and blue dusk was gathering fast.

"And that angel will come in a fiery chariot!"

"Amen!" said Parsons Dreedle just as the little light between the sky and the horizon grew larger.

A few sharp-eyed people took note of it and stirred uneasily, but Claude went tight on, oblivious. "The world will be covered with darkness at the end!"

And the light grew larger and seemed to float across the marsh.

"But there will be one light! And one light only!" Claude continued, so wrapped up in his preaching that he was oblivious to the way people weren't even listening to him anymore, but staring and pointing at the light that was coming toward us; it just seemed to float right over the marsh, like something that was flying, like....

"Like an angel!" Miss Sister Gibbs muttered, squinting into the twilight and crossing her arms over her chest.

I'll give us this: no one panicked or started a stampede; we all just stood there with our mouths full of half-chewed hot dogs and unswallowed soft drinks, watching that light float across the now darkened marsh, gently, slowly moving toward us.

If this is the Angel of the End of the World, then I guess we'll offer him a piece of seven-layer cake and a can of Caffeine Free Diet Pepsi. If it is the end of the world as we know it, at least we'll go out the way we came in. I can't imagine that the next world will have a seven-layer cake any better than the one you get right here in Oysterback.